White Lights, Dark Magic

Cathy Wood Newman

WHITE LIGHTS, DARK MAGIC

www.bluebayoubreeze.com

This work contains pure fiction, any coincidences are precisely coincidence.

DEDICATION

I wouldn't be myself without first and foremost thanking God who blessed me with the ability to capture my imagination on paper.

Thank you for your support and love, to my husband, family, friends and co-workers who always believed in me, especially my mom and dad who is smiling in heaven!

And to my new friends and editors Jerry and Elizabeth, y'all were a fountain of information.

Table of Contents

CHAPTER ONE
Unusual Encounters
New Orleans 1984

My tummy felt stretched from my early dinner at Mother's Diner, the famous eatery downtown New Orleans. I stepped out onto the hot sidewalk as the glass door swung closed behind me. My smile faded as my forehead tingled. I felt as if someone tickled me with a feather. My name, Arielle, was whispered in the winds. I recalled the same feeling at my first encounter with the Voodoo Queen, Miranda LaTour, about three years ago.

During that time, I was doing palm reading on the outskirts of Jackson Square. Coaxed by a bunch of silly high school girls, we tried to make a little extra cash. The tourists loved the lure of a palm reader. I found I possessed an uncanny knack of being very accurate. Miranda lurked around our makeshift tables as we took turns telling fortunes, not realizing we were in any real danger.

Hearing stories about Miranda had made me question how far she would push to get what she wanted. One story that struck a chord about Miranda was a girl named Jenny who graduated several years ahead of me. As I was walked home from my best friend Dixie's house one evening, I spotted Jenny ahead of me. She was stumbling home from an evening in the French Quarter partying with her friends. A dark figure followed her as Jenny ducked down one of the alleys. I followed out of curiosity. Peeking down the alley as I cling to a damp brick wall of the building, I saw Jenny was cornered by Miranda!

"Vieux Carré, make it mine today," Miranda chanted in her raspy voice, black mist floating out of her fingertips and swirling towards Jenny. The mist covered Jenny's eyes, blinding her as it wandered into her gaping mouth. Miranda commanded the mist to return to her, and it pulled Jenny's light purple soul out of her. As it floated towards Miranda, she chanted, "Restore unto me, the youth that flees, my beauty shall always be.

"Stop!" I hollered.

She spun around, blood red eyes piercing me as I felt a jolt of electricity flowing through my body. A hiss escaped her mouth with such volume I covered my ears and fell forward to my knees. White smoke filled the alley.

I scrambled back calling, "Jenny? Are you there?"

The smoke started to clear. Jenny was slumped on the ground. There was no sign of Miranda. I ran to her and gently touched her shoulder. A low groan came from Jenny. *At least she is alive!* She gingerly sat up with her long thick blonde locks draped across her face. I let out a gasp, as she swept them away.

"What?" Jenny exclaimed.

"Your face." I whispered.

"What is wrong with my face?" She said in a panic, patting it.

"Um. Well. You are old." I said trying to gently say the truth.

Her high pitch squeal as she traced the deep wrinkles echoed in my memory.

I attempted to brush away the memory and the lingering feeling on my forehead with a vigorous rub of my index finger. My breath quickened as my eyes shifted, scanning the area, looking up at a sturdy brick building, then to the street examining the people milling around. Picking up the pace, I continued down the zig zag patterned brick sidewalk while glancing over my right shoulder.

I didn't see anything out of the ordinary, but my chest began to tighten, and the suspense started to set in. If not Miranda it was a message of words that someone just needs to hear, or sometimes it was a forewarning. That day I couldn't tell which one it was, but one thing I did know, I couldn't shake the feeling until my task was completed.

Frustrated, I felt compelled to board the streetcar at Canal Street. *Perfect timing*, I said to myself as one eased up to the stop. I waited until I was the last person to board, pausing at the platform my chest tightened as a freezing blast of air parted the stringy hair on the back of my head, slapping the sides of my face. Pressing the coins in the slot nervous about turning around, my eyes rested on the conductor instead. I tried to ignore the odd, frigid air on such a hot, humid day, but I just couldn't.

I pivoted, slowly to look behind me as the grinding doors of the streetcar were closing. Miranda appeared in her all-black attire on the side of the street. My eyes widened in surprise; flushed seeing her. Sucking air in quickly, I held my breath as the streetcar swayed to the left, moving forward. As I peeked through the glass panel doors her long black nails were curled, but one finger pointed straight at me. I could barely see her light chocolate face under the black lace veil until the winds swirled around her, raising the veil. Her brow furrowed and her top lip raised, showing her white teeth next to her ruby red lips. Her growl floated over to me, echoing in my ears. My eyes fluttered. I grabbed hold of the silver bar next to the stairs, trying to shake away the dizziness. Hearing the steady groan of the streetcar on the metal tracks, I exhaled in relief as Miranda faded out of sight.

"Get to it, darling." The heavyset woman conductor with large blond ringlets against her dark black skin urged me to find a seat. Nodding, I moved to find the soul that urge me to board the streetcar.

As I rocked down the aisle with the motion of the car, I held back my straight, strawberry blond hair with my left hand with my head still down, glancing to the side, I looked at the people in their seats. I heard music booming from the rectangle box resting on a guy's shoulder. Playing a little too loud, he pursed his lips and bounced his head forward to the beat. I smiled a little, watching his large, fluffy black hair move to the beat of the music on each be-bop he made. *Nope, it's not him.* I passed up the empty seats near him continuing towards the middle of the streetcar.

The canal streetcar continued to rock on the tracks as it headed for the next stop. *Where are you?* I shouted in my head. I used my right hand to grab hold of the next seat and plopped down. *You need to give me some guidance here!* I tried to clear my thoughts as I looked at my hands and studied my nails. The hot pink polish showed chips all around the edges. I folded my hands in to avoid distraction and asked for God's white light to guide me. I listened for an answer or a sign.

My forehead continued to tingle as I felt a gentle push. Placing my arm on the back of the wooden-slatted bench, I turned my body to view the man behind me. He stared out the window of the streetcar, tinted yellow from all the newly fallen pollen. Lost in his daze, I examined the deep wrinkle in his forehead revealing his concern.

I fanned my open palm close to my face in a short wave. "I'm sorry to bother you." Interrupting his gaze, I felt the soft touch of a woman's hand brush my warm cheek.

"Do you have a wife that has passed?" I asked quietly, not wanting the other passengers to hear our conversation. He blinked hard. Slowly, as the corners of his lips turned down, he created a deep-rooted frown. He turned his eyes; they met mine. I could see the sorrow behind his glossy tears. It felt raw. He remained silent.

A vision flashed in my mind as I continued to speak. "I'm sorry for your loss, but she wants me to tell you to not worry about the small stuff. The kids will be fine... and that you need to remember the good times. Share with the children. Also, when you found the silverware not in order the other day, that was her telling you that everything doesn't need to be perfect."

I held my breath for his response since he had not uttered a single word. A single tear dropped from his eye and landed on his tanned skin. He nodded, looking down where the tear landed. The message was released and so was I. Just a short message this time.

Hearing the ding of the streetcar's bell, I got up, squeezed his arm near where the tear had landed, and made a quick exit. Not knowing the location of the stop, I bounced down the steps and looked left and right to get my surroundings.

Where should I go now? I asked myself as I started walking down Dumaine street. Keenly aware of the people around me, I half expected to see Miranda again. A sense of uneasiness lingered after seeing her, but my forehead felt normal again. I convinced myself she was gone for now.

Out of habit, my left hand rested on my front pocket. Yep, it was still there, my trusty boogieman spray. Not being old enough to own a gun, my papa gave me boogieman spray on my sixteenth

4

birthday. He didn't really elaborate on everything that was in the container, but I probably wouldn't have even paid much attention either.

I lectured myself in my dad's voice. *New Orleans can be an unsafe place for a single young woman. This isn't just any boogieman spray; it has special powers. Remember that!* I nodded and agreed with him. As I strolled down the brick sidewalk, I thought, *I probably threw in a slight eye roll at the end of our conversation.*

Luckily, I have not used this spray concoction that he bestowed upon me before he passed away, but I always kept it close by. It was a comfort to remember his goofy sense of humor... boogieman spray. It made me laugh at the absurdity.

Feeling much safer for the moment, I realized I wasn't too far from Central Grocery where I could pick up a few things for the house.

And now, after making my purchases, I held the brown paper grocery bag with both arms as I walked over towards Royal Street. The sun began to dip down as the flicker of the gas lanterns light posts cast light shadows that danced on the old two-story buildings. The heat of the day still radiated off the pavement, creating a wave in one's vision along with the darkness, making a very haunting setting.

There sat a large dog two houses down from my home. *That's a shame. Someone lost their pet. I wonder if he has a collar?* Squinting a little in the darkening evening, I slowed my pace to see him better. He watched as I crossed the street towards my front door. The dog rose from his sitting position and stood to face me; he was all black. He looked almost like a shadow. His lips curled around his yellow teeth as a low growl bounced off the buildings. He moved swiftly across the street.

Starting to panic now, I grabbed for my key to unlock the door. The beast took a full leap towards me. As he bit down on my left wrist, I yelped from the pain of his teeth burrowing into my flesh. I swung at the animal and he released, only to bite again. I moved my arm out of the way as his teeth grabbed hold of my boogieman spray. The container exploded from my jeans pocket with a brilliant ray of white light. The dog turned into a silver liquid that pooled, draining over my jeans and evaporating before it hit the ground.

Frantically, I looked up and around me to see if anyone else had witnessed this event. I was all alone. Fussing into the evening sky, "What the hell was that? Why are you not protecting me? Are you even there, Papa?"

I examined my wrist, looking for bite marks, but there were none. Instead a red glowing burn mark pulsed. Gingerly I tapped it with my right index finger, noticing how tender it felt. With my vision blurred, my bottom lip pushed out as my eyes filled with tears. I steadied my hand to unlock the front door. Relieved I forgot to turn the light out they cast out of the house as I stooped down and worked on retrieving my dropped bag. Disgusted, I just left the glass jar of jelly shattered on the sidewalk and the colorful orange satsumas that had rolled out onto the street.

Once secure in my home, I put my head down on the mahogany kitchen table, letting myself cry. The emotions from losing my dad just a few months ago to cancer and the frightful things happening were too much to bear. I needed a friend. I needed someone I could trust to confide in. I wanted my mama.

*****

The powerful sounds of the deep ring of the kitchen phone echoed up the stairs into the hallway connected to my room. I dragged myself out of bed to cross the room and picked up the receiver in my bedroom. Having my ringer turned off didn't make much difference with the old wall mount phone mama had in the kitchen. My voice cracked out a low, "Hellooo"

"Hi, sweetie, I just wanted to check in on you and see how you are doing." The comforting sounds of my mama's voice made a smile cross my face.

With a slow, sad-sounding response, I cradled the phone close to my ear, so wishing she was home to give me one of her warm hugs. "All right, Mama."

6

"What is the matter?"

Sighing, I said, "Nothing. I was sleeping."

"I can hear it in your voice! Are you doing okay, Arielle?" She pressed for me to spill what was really bothering me.

Trying to change my voice to not be so mopey; I dropped a little white lie. "I just had a rough couple of nights' sleep, that's all." I twisted the spiral phone cord in my index finger, waiting to see if she bought it.

"Oh sweetie, I am sorry. I wish I was there, but I will be home soon! It may be only a few more weeks. Are you having bad dreams again?"

Rubbing the sleep out of one eye, I offered up a little more information. "I am just missing you and Papa. I feel very alone right now."

"I miss him too." I could hear her voice crack a little. "I feel so bad leaving you with all this so fresh. I have a few more things to take care of and I am coming back home, I promise."

Her voice switched gears. "Oh, I wanted to ask you. Are you registered for your fall classes?"

"Uh, well... not exactly," I stammered, shaking my head with a slight eye roll.

"Arielle, you know you need to register. Once you take a break, it is so hard to get back into going to school. Remember your plan. You want to graduate in three more years." Mama's voice came across the phone with a sharp sternness.

"I know, Mama, I know," I rolled my eyes again. "Look, I gotta go."

Mama backed down from the conversation, saying, "Okay, sweetie. I will call you in a few days, and I should know by then when I am taking a flight back home. Aunt Mabel wanted me to tell you hello, and she wished you had made the trip up to Michigan to visit. I told her maybe next time. Make sure to check the answering machine if I miss you when I call, but I can take a cab home from the airport if I need to. I love you, Arielle."

"I love you too. Tell Aunt Mabel I said hello, and I will come next summer for the next family reunion." I gave the phone a thumbs up as if Mama could see me.

I gently placed my mustard yellow receiver back on the wall, my forehead pressed against the phone as I thought about the conversation. Speaking to the empty phone, I moaned, "Blah, I don't want to be in school right now."

The unexpected ringing of the phone caused me to jump back as I snatched it up and pressed it to my ear. "Hello?"

"One more thing I forgot to tell you. There is a book your papa left. I keep forgetting to tell you about it."

"Summer reading?" I asked casually.

"Not exactly. It is in our closet in a wooden box, a locked leather-bound book. I don't have a key, but he said you wouldn't need a key."

"That's weird, but... okay, thanks. I will check it out. Do you know what the book is about? Did he leave one for Mark too?" I asked as my mind wandered with many questions.

"He never really talked much about the content of the book. But he did tell me that you would need it later in life. Your papa was always into something different. No, Papa only left you a book, not your brother. Maybe the book will make you feel a little better having something close that he made just for you. I will let you go. I love you, Arielle. Bye for now."

"Thanks, I love you too." My hand was still on the receiver when the phone rang a third time. "What did you forget this time, Mama?"

I could hear a gurgling sound on the other end of the phone. "Hello?"

A low sound of a man's voice came through on the phone. "Gris-gris is all around you."

8

"Whatever, weirdo!" I slammed the phone down. *Creepy guy,* I thought to myself. *Why would someone call and say that? Was he trying to put a hex on me?* Living in south Louisiana, a lot of unexplained things occur. Voodoo, dark magic, and spells were all very alive and real in my world. Growing up Catholic, we were warned about the dangers but not educated about them.

I was in Mama's closet on my tiptoes pulling down boxes from the shelf when the phone rang again. Letting the answering machine get it, I continued to search for the book. I felt around with my fingertips until I discovered a wooden box.

Trying to pull it closer, a sliver of wood jabbed into my index finger. I snapped my hand back to see a little mark where the wood was lodged into my skin. Ugh! After freeing my finger from the painful little prick, I padded downstairs to find the step stool. The red light on the answering machine was blinking at me. Someone had left a message. With the small wooden stool in one hand, I pressed the button and started walking back towards the stairs.

The first message was Mark. "Hey, Arielle, I haven't heard from you in a few days. Call me back." He must have phoned when I was at Dixie's house visiting for a few days. I am not too fond of staying in this big house all alone, so I tended to stay with friends.

The last message I heard as I climbed the stairs was the same man's voice. "Gris-gris is all around you," he growled.

Shaking my head in disgust, I wringed my hands as I continued back into Mama's bedroom to locate the book. As I approached the closet, a soft ice blue glow came from the doorway. I paused for a moment, then cautiously crept to hug the doorframe and peeked inside. The color snapped out of view as the room appeared to be the normal color under the dull yellowish light bulb.

Placing the stool firmly on the ground, I stepped up to look at the wooden box. The sides of the box had a low glow of the same blue color. Placing my hands around the box, the color brightened. *This was insane.* When I moved my hands away, the color faded. Fixated, I lifted the brightly illuminated box, stepped off the stool, and walked to the roll top corner desk. Once my hands released the box, the color disappeared completely.

I was a little nervous about opening it. Placing my finger tips on the lid the light pulsed mimicking my rapid heartbeat. The flashing color filled my eyes, fading my fears, and inviting me to open it. The hinge on the box made a small squeak when as I slowly opened the lid. A leather-bound book was inside with a symbol burned on the front. I ran my fingertips across the logo, examining it, trying to remember if I had seen it before. The thick outside circle had a horizontal line through the middle with what appeared to be the top part of a "C" above the line and below the shape of a "V".

I turned the book on its side. There was a small padlock that required a key. I put the book on the desk and searched in the box for a key, but I only found several spray bottles of boogieman spray and one tiny amber glass bottle labeled hyssop oil. I struggled to pry the book open with my hands; a few stray lines of white light escaped from the pages and gave me a small jolt of electricity, causing me to drop the book on the hard floor with a loud *thunk*.

Gently, I picked up the book, turned it around in my hands and examined the lock closely. I could smell the pages of the old book. *Could I snip the lock with a pair of wire cutters? Wouldn't hurt to try, right??*

I put the book back in the box and placed all the other items back in Mama's closet, keeping an extra spray bottle out to carry with me. Rolling my eyes, I thought, *Without a key I'm not sure what Papa was thinking.*

Rummaging through mama's jewelry making kit I found the cutters. As I held cold metal clippers in my right hand, the lock dangled from the book as the two drew closer together. The book started to jolt and caused my arm to violently shake. I pressed the book down on the nightstand using the weight of my body, and the clippers opened wide to clamp down on the lock. The light blast escaping from the book sent me airbone, the clippers clattered onto the floor as I landed square on my butt.

Gathering everything I stomped back into my bedroom tossing everything on my unmade bed. Flexing my empty hand, I turned my focus on the book. My head shook in disgust. I hid the book in the box on the floor of my closet and closed the slatted door. Blue lines of color filled my room reminding me the book was there waiting for me to open it.

Leaning against the wall next to my closet, I reflected on what to do next. I heard the attic creaking as the blue color turned into a deep red color then faded away. "I miss you, Papa," I spoke softly, looking up towards the ceiling. The sounds of a child giggling and bouncing a ball in the attic echoed above me. I didn't feel like dealing with any supernatural encounters right now. The ghosts constantly rotated in our home. Some, not peaceful, entered our home often, and I didn't want to find out which one this would be. I needed to get out of this house and find a healthy distraction.

CHAPTER TWO
Sprinkle Some Fun

Escaping the possible encounter with the spirit in the attic, I stepped outside. The sun shone bright as hot winds swirled violently around me and lifted my hair to slap me in the face. Hearing a low cry circling my head, I stopped my short walk and moved closer to the next building. I pressed my eyes closed to avoid being stung by my hair.

The sounds I heard were the sounds of the spirits talking to each other, but I did not understand their language. The spirits were gathering a soul about to be released to them. I placed my hands across my forehead with my elbows extended outward and let the sounds fill my ears. It's a sad time for us when a loved one dies. A voice filled my head, saying the traditional things that surround death. *They are in a better place. It will be easier with time.*

But what about the gaping hole in my heart? I pondered.

The voice continued, *When someone passes, this is a joyful time because we received someone else to live eternally with us and with our God.*

As the sounds became quiet and the voice drifted away, my eyes popped open and shifted rapidly to scan the area. I noticed the couple across the street. The woman was leaning against the painted brick wall with one leg propped up. The man, wearing a black derby hat, had her giggling about something he whispered to her as he leaned into her ear. I moved my gaze down the uneven sidewalk and saw that no one was walking towards me. I listened to the clip-clop sounds of the horse and buggy passing, eavesdropping on the tour guide pointing out the French influences on the buildings around us as I came closer to Jackson Square.

An unseasonably cool breeze blew by my face. I began to smell something, similar to old clothes. It reminded me of my grandmother's house. It was funny how the spirits talked to me through my senses. Following the breeze toward the sky, I saw a vision of a white dove flying above me. It quickly flew out of sight.

A wedding! I exclaimed to myself. I love it when I remember the symbols that were shown to me. I smiled, thinking *I might be just getting the hang of this stuff!* I noticed a woman wearing a lace charcoal shawl. She was very close to me, only an arm's length away, facing away from me. There were several people around us now; everyone but her walked with a purpose down Pirate's Alley located next to Jackson Square. She remained very still. I had a strong feeling the message I received actually was intended for this woman who studied the buildings.

"Excuse me, ma'am," I said to her, reaching out to tap her. Still not sure if I should be touching her, I held back, with my right arm slightly outreached. "I believe I have a message to deliver to you." She had not yet turned towards me, but she did stop looking up at the buildings. I could only see the back of her head. Her gray hair matched the color of the shawl draped over her narrow shoulders. The thick lines of grays intertwined, creating a full head of wiry hair. "I know this might sound strange, but did you ever try on your grandmother's wedding dress?"

She rotated on her heels slowly to face me. As I looked into her eyes, I noticed they were red as blood with no pupils. She retorted, "Maybe that message is actually for you?" She drew her upper lip into a snarl, showing her stark white shark-like teeth.

Confused by what I saw, I stumbled backwards on the uneven pavement and flailed my arms to keep my balance. Unaware of anyone else around us, I only focused on her eyes and didn't really comprehend that she had even spoken.

"I know that you used to try on your grandmother's wedding dress," she said in a low, scratchy voice. As she leaned towards me, I pulled my arms into my chest, and my right shoulder pushed up to the sky to try to shield my face. In full view I could see her face was a grayish color, but not as dark as her hair, creating a slight contrast and displaying her deep wrinkles.

My eyes blinking rapidly, my mind raced, and I thought to myself, *Although that is true, how could she know that? Or is that a common thing that little girls do?* I finally stammered to her, "I--I--apologize for having bothered you." I continued backing away from her.

Her eyes fixated on me as she advanced. I continued to move backwards, staying just out of her reach. "But don't you want to hear your message, young lady?" she whispered in a sweet tone that turned low and harsh as she pressed her head into her body, "You think you're so great, running around this town telling everyone your messages. Who do you think you are? Well, I've got news for you about this little gift you have. You don't even know how to use it, and now I'm going to take it from you."

My face felt cool as the blood drained away and fear took over. I tried hard to swallow, but the dryness in my throat made it impossible. She lunged, stomping her right foot and extending her left arm, snatching at me in a scooping motion as a dark mist began to surround us. I managed to squeeze to the side, pulling away from her grasp.

Swatting at the mist with my left arm, I struggled to get the new boogieman spray out of my pocket. Face to face, the mist enclosed us as I extended my arms out straight and pushed down on the trigger. A stream of liquid shot out, directly hitting the decrepit woman in her forehead and dripping down to her nose. She let out an ear-piercing howl and cupped her face with her hands as her flesh began to melt, exposing her skull and finger bones. I spun and used my spray again; the mist evaporated. I bolted away, plowing through a couple's romantic stroll and parting them like the Red Sea. They yelled after me, "Excuse you!" I never looked back.

Darting through Jackson Square and crossing Decatur Street, I jogged up the stairs then down to the moonwalk by the river. I slowed down to catch my breath. Taking a moment, I glanced behind me to see a few tourist wandering around aimlessly.

14

I began to doubt it was even real; no one else seems to witness these things happening to me. *Am I crazy? Did any of that just happen?* Leaning against the streetcar stop booth, I gasped in some air as I tried to catch my breath. I looked around one last time and stepped aboard the streetcar heading towards Esplanade Avenue.

What in the heck just happened? I wondered as I sat down. A vision of Miranda popped into my head. She was behind all of this! *These dark spirits normally only came around in the nighttime, but they seem to now be appearing all the time.* Examining the bite mark from the other night, it now glowed a deep red and the welts had returned. I placed my hand over the area and asked the white lights to be with me and protect me since I had no idea what to do to keep myself safe. Certainly, boogieman spray would not be the answer to keeping the spirits at bay. I had to do some research and figure out what needed to be done to keep the dark spirits in check! I didn't know who to ask for help, but maybe if I could get that book open from Papa, I could get some answers.

I was very lost and confused as I asked the spirits my recurring questions. *Okay, spirits, where should I go? What should I do? Can you give me a clue how to get Papa's book open?* The silence indicated they were not going to give me any clear direction. *How could I push all of this aside and just resume a normal life?* I figured the next best thing was to visit my best friend, Dixie. She would help me put my mind at ease. I pulled hard on the overhead string, creating the "ding ding" sound of the bell instructing the conductor to halt at the next stop. I hopped off at the French Market stop, crossed the North St. Peter's Street, and jogged down Esplanade Avenue until I saw the navy-blue trim on Dixie's house.

When I arrived, her mom, DeeDee, was sitting on the porch with a glass of amber sweet tea in her hand. She rocked in her wicker chair, enjoying the day and watching people pass by. Her large brown sunglasses covered most of her dark tan face. Her bright teal shirt created an intense contrast against her olive skin. She saw me and gave a wave as her gold and silver bangle bracelets jingled.

"Hi, Ms. DeeDee," I called, a little out of breath from the jog, while I used both hands to open the latch on the short black rod iron gate to their front yard.

Slowly walking up the terra cotta steps to her home, I heard Ms. DeeDee chattering to me, "Hi, darling, you back again so soon? Why were you running? It is way too hot for such a foolish thing. Would you like something cold to drink?"

"Yes, ma'am, I would. Is Dixie home?" I responded, standing in front of her on the small porch. She lifted the pitcher covered in condensation from the heat of the day and poured a glass for me.

"Yes, she is home and is studying the schedule book figuring out her classes for next semester." she told me, "I assume you have your schedule already figured out?"

"Thank you. Oh, yes, I know exactly what I want to do next semester," I told Ms. DeeDee, but thinking, *I want to skip this semester!* I took a deep breath and began to tilt my head back and almost drank all the sweet tea out of the glass. I took in a deep breath as the back of my hand wiped away any excess tea that didn't make it into my mouth.

"Let me refill that for you." She reached for the glass and handed it back full again. "Well, head on inside. I'm sure she could use a little break." She shooed me with her hand pointing towards the front door.

With the fresh glass in hand, I walked inside and plopped down next to Dixie, almost spilling some of my drink. She glanced up, looking a little annoyed.

"What's up?" she asked quickly. I put my hand over her book so she couldn't read and held my glass towards the ceiling. Looking up at me, she had a look of total annoyance. Her face changed quickly, "Are you okay?"

"Not really I am creeped out by some stuff that is happening, I need to get my mind off of it for a bit."

"Come on, let's roll!" She said with a giggle, dropping her pencil.

"Where are we going?" I asked with a sigh taking sip from my drink.

"Someplace new and exciting, the World's Fair!" She exclaimed!

My face lit up as she scooted off the bed. She grabbed her mustard yellow helmet from her closet. Her mom didn't like the idea of us on the motorcycle, but she was warming up to the idea because, she didn't really have much of a choice.

We bounced out of the house and darted down Royal Street towards Esplanade Avenue to get the red Kawasaki 1100 motorcycle parked in my courtyard a few blocks away. Before Ms. DeeDee even had time to object, I placed the empty glass on the table as I scurried by. "Thanks for the cool drink, Ms. DeeDee!"

Dixie hollered from the street, "We are going to check out the World's Fair and will be back before dark." Dixie knew I didn't like to be out after dark. We soon had our helmets on and were flying down the road in no time. We could have walked to the fair, but this was much more fun.

Steering the bike with Dixie holding onto my waist, I maneuvered into a small spot under a large oak tree close to the entrance. Hanging our helmets on the handlebars, Dixie said, "Excellent parking spot!" with a thumbs up.

We approached the grand entrance just a short distance away. Hand-painted alligators carved out of some kind of material loomed above us, casting long shadows. "This is amazing!" I said. Dixie agreed with a slow, steady nod, taking it all in with her eyes wide and mouth slightly parted in awe.

Dixie grabbed my arm and pointed at the sculpted mermaid. Her tail was about twenty feet long. "That is so cool," she said as she twirled around. "Ah, the life of a mermaid. Can you imagine?"

"I think I would be a giant prune if I was in the water all the time."

"Oh Arielle, where is your imagination?" she chuckled.

We made our way past the entrance and saw a brightly colored sign stating, 'kids' car wash'. *Man, we didn't bring our bathing suits!* I thought to myself. Large rainbow-colored wheels covered in the soft flowing materials gently flung water like a car wash. The sounds of kids giggling and screaming filled the air. We glanced at each other, both thinking the same thing at the same time.

Taking off running towards the kid wash, we ran through it, laughing our heads off. Once we made it out the other side, the laughing continued for several minutes. Refreshed from cool water, we could see the heat radiating off the cement distorting our vision. I pointed and laughed at her hair plastered to her head, and she did the same to me. Our wet footprints evaporated immediately as we walked further into the fair.

We stumbled upon a woman wearing a pink kimono dress as a crowd formed around her. Peeking around the people who gathered in front of me, I could see her stark white-painted face and ruby red lips. Her arms reached out from under of her long flowing sleeves. Orchestrating two women in white glistening leotards posed with their long sticks and bright red ribbons attached to them. Holding the sticks as far as they could reach in the sky, the motion started slowly, causing a ripple effect until all the ribbon was airborne. In unison, they started twirling the ribbons around them, creating shapes and curly Q's. As they skipped around the women in pink, the ribbons trailed out long and flowing, creating an occasional snap sound with a flip of their wrists. It was so beautiful to watch, almost mesmerizing to see.

The two women twirled off and disappeared back into the crowd, leaving the woman in pink standing alone. We erupted in applause with a few stray whistles of approval. She joined her hands together as if in prayer, bowing forward at the waist. Back upright, she walked into the crowd, and they parted, allowing her passage.

"How amazing was that?" I asked Dixie. "What talent. Can you imagine if you could do flips like that? Talk about being in the right place at the right time too!"

The aggravating feeling returned as we continued exploring the fair. I slowed my pace and came to a halt as I rubbed at my forehead. Dixie stopped as well to turn and look at me. She knew something was happening to me.

I was beginning to think this was more of a curse because it always intruded on my life and my plans. I just wish I knew how to make the most of this since it is apparently not going away. With my pinky finger turned up, I used my three fingers and began to tap on my forehead, releasing a loud sigh.

CHAPTER THREE
Bird's Eye View

"Something is happening, isn't it? You are rubbing your head again." I nodded as she waited for me to hone in on who, in the thin crowd around us, was my next client. I walked up to a boy and his family. "May I speak with your son?" His mother wrapped her left arm across the front of the boy, giving me a sideways glance. "I am able to talk to spirits that have passed on, and a mother or grandmother figure is trying to communicate."

Before his parents could even object, the boy said, "My grandmother died not too long ago. But I don't really remember much of her."

Leaning over to look at the boy's deep blue eyes, I said, "She is telling me about a dark-colored dog."

He chimed, "I had a chocolate lab!"

"Your grandmother is saying something to do with the number nine."

His eyes widened as he glanced at his mother, "Buster, my chocolate lab, died, and he was nine years old. We were the same age. This is so freaky!"

Each experience leaves me in awe with the power that spirits could communicate with a simple person like myself. "Your grandmother wants you to know that Buster is with her and he is healthy and happy. He wants you to know how much he loves you and knows how much you cared for him in the end."

The boy's bottom lip quivered as he used the back of his hand to wipe away a few stray tears and ran them on his pants to dry off. His parents gave a round of applause, thinking I was part of the World's Fair entertainment. Extending my arm to the side, I took a bow and walked away to blend into the crowd with Dixie right on my heels.

We spotted a white pelican dressed in a powder blue top hat and matching jacket. A large five-inch button pinned on the lapel said, 'Seymour D. Fair.' "Ha! Get it? See more da fair? That is his name!" I said as I tapped my finger on the button.

A loud rumble intruded on my exciting development. We both looked from above to each other, knowing that we were thinking the same thing. We followed the tracks in the sky to find where we could board the monorail.

On our way, we stopped to pick up a New Orleans style snowball to help cool us off in the scorching heat. The temperature with the heat index could easily have been 100 degrees. Unlike snowcones or slushies found in the rest of the country, our local snowballs are created from ice shaved so fine it is like powder then topped off with any flavor you could imagine. I always chose spearmint, but it would turn my tongue green--a small downside to getting that flavor, but it was so worth it. Giggling from a sugar high, we passed a few exhibits on our way to the monorail.

"We have to stop and check this out. They have a full-size space shuttle over there!" Dixie squealed and tugged on my arm as I tried to balance my snowball from the jolt. "You know I always wanted to be an astronaut when we were kids. I can't believe they have a real shuttle here. And it's the Enterprise shuttle too!"

"I didn't realize how big this thing is," I said with my mouth slightly open because my head was tilted back trying to view the top.

A very young girl with red ringlets patted her dad's shirt. "Daddy, I want to be an astronaut one day," she said, pointing at the white shuttle. "I could fly one of those in outer space and battle aliens."

Placing my hand over the side of my mouth, I whispered to Dixie, "I have enough unknown things here on this earth. I don't think I would like to go into space. There might be even more creepy things out there!"

"I bet there is some really creepy stuff out there that they are not telling us about, like super aliens!" she said as she tossed her brown hair and wrinkled her nose at me.

My tongue peeked out and made a fart noise at her as I rolled my eyes. "Come on, let's keep going."

Stumbling upon the entrance to a plaza, I stopped to read a plaque. In a monotone voice I recapped what the sign said. "You are located in Centennial Plaza. The last world's fair in New Orleans was called the Cotton Fair. It was 100 years ago."

I closed my eyes to imagine the men, women, and children walking around in their fancy clothing that I would never wear, and they must have been so hot in all those long, flowing dresses. Shifting gears to something more my speed, my eyes popped open to glance at Dixie. "I wonder what kind of "carnie" food would they have had? Do you think they had kettle corn 100 years ago?"

"Kettle corn was created around 1776." She pressed her index finger to her lips, looking up, thinking hard, "and I think it was the Dutch, but I can't be sure about that part."

"Really? No way! How do you retain that random crap?" I laughed as we navigated through the crowds.

"I pay attention more than you do." She said. I stuck my green tongue out at her, and she retorted with her purple tongue as we laughed.

"Look, a Ferris wheel. We can ride it to the top and see where the monorail starts!" I pointed directly head of us. "We can do this together. You need to conquer this fear anyway, right?" I pressed a dollar into the hand of the worker, pulling Dixie towards the seats as she shook her head saying no. I kept her mind occupied chattering about recent events that were happening to me.

"I want to show you the book papa left for me."

"That is a fantastic idea," Dixie said as the ride ended, "Oh, thank God that is over! Now let's go do the monorail."

"Thanks for humoring me. You know I love the Ferris wheel."

"You are lucky I like you!" She said winking at me.

Sounds echoed from kids squealing from either fear or delight as we weaved through several dozen carnival rides. Finally, we found the monorail. It was free, even better! Taking our seats, we looked out the windows at the people milling around below us. *UGH!* My forehead was tingling again. The more people around, the more the spirits call upon me.

I squinted out the window, then over to where Dixie had positioned herself for the best view. A quick shadow flashed across the window; *This high up it could only be a bird*, I reasoned in my head. All of a sudden, our car lurched to the left and a ripple effect of surprised "Oooh's" funneled down the car from the unexpected movement.

Quickly glancing back at the window, a large unidentified gray bird latched onto the window next to Dixie. I fell back out of my seat onto the floor in shock. Scrambling to my feet, but still crouching beneath the window filled with feathers indicating this was a huge bird. It pushed off with its back legs as the claws drug across the Plexiglas, making a dull, steady, scraping sound, causing the cart to wobble again, and I landed on my butt.

All eyes fixed on me to see if I was all right. Chattering people gathered around me asking, "Are you okay?" Dumbfounded, I pointed at the window, but the only thing that remained was the jagged claw marks carved into the window.

Pulling me back in my seat, Dixie shooed everyone away. "She is fine, just a little dizzy from the jolt of the train. Thank you for your concern."

With my head in my palms, I looked up at her pleading, "Please tell me you saw that thing at the window?"

She whispered back to me, "I'm sorry, but I didn't see anything. Everyone including me was watching you on the floor! Do you want to tell me about it?"

"No, but I do have to talk to someone."

"You know you can always talk to me." She looked in my eyes with sincerity mixed with a little hurt that I didn't want to tell her about my experiences.

Staring at Dixie, I drew back my head a little as my eyebrows squished into the top of my eyelids, diverting my gaze away from her. She grabbed my chin, forcing me to look back at her, and asked, "What is it?"

"It's you."

"What about me?" She released my chin, but her hand remained.

"Someone wants to talk to you!"

Snapping her hand back close to her shoulder, she shook her head, "Oh no, you don't!"

"Oh yeah!" I said back to her, "Didn't your grandmother pass from a heart attack?"

She nodded and turned to look out the window, "Do you want me to go on?" I gently asked.
She didn't look back at me, but nodded *yes*.

"She wants you to know how proud she is of you for going to college." This was so crazy for me to read someone I knew so closely in my life. I wasn't ever able to do this, like ever! My index fingernail found its way between my teeth as I began to gnaw off my nail polish. I didn't want to upset Dixie, but I wanted her to have her message. I know she always supported me in my gifts and I didn't think this would change anything. At least I hoped not.

Dixie faced me; there was a single line where tears had rolled down her cheek. "Is there anything else she wants to tell me?" she asked. "And will you stop doing that!" She swatted at the back of my hand.

"I can't help it!" I said, spitting out little pieces of pink polish onto the floor. "Let me see." I closed my eyes, cleared my mind, and took in some deep breathes to see if any other images or feelings came to me. "I felt tightness in my chest, but not an overwhelming sense of pain. She wants you to know she didn't suffer from the heart attack."

"Grandma was in the hospital for about a week after the heart attack and was hooked up to every machine known by man to keep her alive, but she never awoke. A coma-like state is what they called it." Dixie nodded about her memory as the corners of her mouth slightly turned upwards. "I am glad she didn't suffer. I try to recall memories of her, but they seem to fade the older I get. I was only six when she died."

It was my turn to listen to Dixie as she continued, "We met the year after she passed. I didn't talk about her much then, but as new friends at the age of seven, talking about your dead grandmother wasn't a hot topic."

I nodded, remembering her too. "She makes me feel warm, like she was always making cookies and holding you in her arms."

Dixie agreed with this statement with a small nod and a little larger smile. Lost deep in her memories I felt the monorail begin to slow. "Now that I put a damper on today's fun, do you want to get off the monorail and see something else?" I asked with a little shoulder shrug and hands folded together. I waited for an answer.

She rose, not speaking, so I knew her answer was *yes*. Once we winded down the staircase and back onto the hot concrete, I scouted for where to go next. I looped my arm into Dixie's as we wandered over to another ride, the Louisiana history water boat tour. "This looks like it might be boring. You would love it, right?" I said, trying to get a chuckle out of her.

"Sure." We walked over and took a spot in line. We didn't say much, just watched the interesting people of New Orleans walk by. A shadow flashed over us; shielding my eyes with my palm, I looked up. *What the heck kind of bird is that?* Staring up, I examined the options. *Maybe it is gray? The only large bird I could think of was the great blue heron, but the color was wrong. Nothing else from around here would be that size and color.*

Dixie mimicked me gazing up and broke our silent spell. "What are you looking for?"

"There is a bird flying around up there. Remember, I took a bird watching course in high school, but I can't figure out this one. I thought I really knew every bird in Louisiana. I thought it was the same bird that I saw on the monorail, but this is too high in the sky for me to see the size and color of it."

"What bird? I don't see anything," she said, holding her hand up to shield the sun from her eyes to glance around.

But it was gone. "Never mind," I said, shaking my head and wrinkling my nose. "It is no big deal."

I pointed to the gap between us and the people ahead. The line was moving very fast, which was good because it was too hot outside to stand still. My shirt was starting to stick to my skin and my socks felt wet.

Walking into the building, a cold blast of air greeted us at the door. I tugged repeatedly on my shirt to try to release any excess heat from my body. Guided with a hand gesture from a man dressed in a white suit with a blue bow tie, we walked towards the left to stand in another line. Once we sat on the boat, the lights dimmed as the boat rocked and splashed on the motorized track.

A man's deep voice similar to James Earl Jones rambled over the light whirring sound of the boat about the history of Louisiana. I took a moment to close my eyes and just let myself relax. "You enjoy this. I am taking a nap. You can cram more random crap in your head and tell me about it later." The boat bumped back onto a track, jolting me awake.

Leaving the coolness, we emerged into the bright afternoon sun. The heat hit us harder than the music warming up nearby. "Let's go check that out next." I said pointing to the jazz band.

The crowd shook white napkins above their heads, dancing in a line trying to create a "second line". Pausing for a moment, we watched the festivities. I quietly followed Dixie as she wandered off. Finding ourselves by the levee on the Mississippi River, we sat on one of the green iron benches.

"Are you sure about your major?" I asked, trying to get her mind off her grandma.

She nodded yes and looked out at the water. "Yes, I really want to help shape the future of our children, and teaching is how I can achieve this dream."

"I feel so lost. I can't figure out what I am doing from day to day let alone shape the lives of children!"

She laughed, "Arielle, you know God has something grand in store for you!"

"I sure hope He knows what He is doing!" I joked.

Hearing music in the distance, we saw a riverboat chugging in our direction with the calliope playing. The music resembled someone plinking on a piano while blowing a whistle at the same time. My left foot began tapping automatically to the Sinatra song "High Hopes". A crowd gathered for the ten-minute show. Dixie and I rose to clap loudly along with everyone.

"It is starting to get dark," I said. "Can we make our way to the motorcycle? We could always come back. The fair should be here several more months."

Dixie's old high school boyfriend was sitting on the seat of the motorcycle as we strolled up. These two were inseparable in high school; not having much of a love life, I became their third wheel. After graduation Dixie decided to take a break to focus on her studies. Ernie didn't really like that idea, but she didn't give him an option.

I gave them a moment to talk before I walked up to her and tugged on her shirt and said, "I don't want to ride in the dark."

She nodded. They finished up their conversation and gave each other a hug. I gave Ernie a wave and a smile as I put my helmet on and asked Dixie's opinion, "Do you think we have time to run by my house to get that book before the darkness rolls in?"

"I think we do if you make it quick," she said. We pulled up to Dixie's house just as the sun started to dip down under the houses around us. I left my helmet on the handlebars and Dixie took hers off, then handed me my backpack with Papa's book in it.

CHAPTER FOUR
Gone Missing

Mrs. DeeDee had supper on the stove. It smelled yummy even from the porch. It must have been Monday because she had prepared red beans and rice. A staple Monday meal in southern Louisiana.

We could hear Mr. Paul kicking off his heavy boots on the porch just a few minutes after we arrived. He worked at one of the local oil companies, dockside, and was fortunate enough to come home each night. We all sat down at the table, said grace, and dug in.

"Nice to see you again, Arielle," Mr. Paul said to me after his first bite.

"Thank you for having me, again."

"Your mama coming home soon?"

"Yes, she said in a couple of weeks."

"All right then, I hope she is doing well."

"Yes sir, she is."

"You can pay off your meal, by helping Dixie with the cleanup."

"Yes sir, thank you."

Hovering over the sink, I whispered to Dixie, "Should I go home?"

"Why?" she asked as she flicked the tiny bubbles from her hands into the sink.

"Well, your dad seemed a little put out that I was here again, right?" I said, focusing on scrubbing the cream-colored plate with a dark blue rim.

"Nah. He was just making small talk."

"Are you sure?" I asked, glancing at her to see if her face was saying something differently.

"Yes, you are fine. He talks to all those gross men all day, so he fumbles for what to say with small talk. He just wanted to make sure you are doing okay with your mama gone. That is all. Trust me, I have lived with him long enough to know him."

"Okay, I just wanted to make sure I wasn't overextending my welcome here."

"Just shut up and let's finish the dishes. So, we can get in our Pjs faster."

Dixie pulled out the bed hiding under hers. Giving the lever a tug, it popped up to meet her bed. Digging in her closet, she tossed me a pillow and pink blanket with small hearts that was resting on the top shelf.

Once we were in our pajamas and staring at the small shadows on the popcorn ceiling cast from her bedside lamp, she asked me, "How do you do it?"

"Do what?"

"Talk to complete strangers. Don't you worry they might be weirdos or maybe freak out on you?"

"I do worry about those things a lot, and it happens to me too! I must tell people what the spirits want them to know, otherwise they annoy the crap out of me until I do it. I am still working on my system to decipher what they are trying to say to me."

I was so glad I had a loyal friend that I trusted. "I have been accused of "fishing" for information to make it look like I am a fraud." My mind wandered back... "Voodoo is the work of the devil!" the Catholic priest would warned from the pulpit. And if it is of the devil you just stay far away from it. Basically, I was taught we don't want to learn about it, just stay away from it.

"Tell me a story, Arielle, so I can fall asleep."

"Mama would take us to Sunday mass at St. Louis Cathedral. If we collectively could answer her questions about the holy message that week, we would walk over to Cafe Du Monde for beignets and coffee with chicory of course. That warm square doughnut covered in powder sugar was enough to make even the atheist pay attention!

Mark and I, along with any of the foster kids, or as my Papa called them, strays, currently living with us would have a good time with the sugar. Just make sure no one makes you inhale while you are trying the first bite, a snort of powdered sugar doesn't go down so well! Or a fake sneeze towards a stray is always a fun trick. Being a Deacon at the church, Papa dressed his best every Sunday and would skip out on the sugary goodness. One full bite instantly covered you in sugar and licking it off didn't remove it. You would just become a sticky mess.

Mama kept the gumbo on the stove on low, so when we got home, the house smelled like one of those fine restaurants downtown with an expensive chef chopping and cutting to make one of the famous New Orleans dishes. She would start preparing early in the morning before service with a roux. This takes time and love to simmer down equal parts oil and flour, constantly stirring until the mixture becomes the color of an old penny. The strays would take turns stirring because you don't want to burn the roux.

Next was the "holy trinity" bell peppers, onions, and celery all diced up. She could cut up an onion without shedding a tear. She had become so immune to it over the years of dicing. Of course, we learned that no gumbo would be complete without Andouille sausage and all the lingering leftovers from the week were added to the pot. Mama learned to stretch the food in our home since there were always new foster kids staying at our house each year. Mark and I always picked up new friends whose home life wasn't so great, and they stayed with us on and off in high school.

Our meals were fairly routine in our home; Monday was red beans and rice. Next to the pot of gumbo she had the beans for Monday soaking. This was an easy meal and gave her time to work on the laundry for the week." The sounds of Dixie's deep breathing interrupted my story time. Tugging the covers up to my neck, I rolled over, letting sleep take over.

A distant drum roll disrupted my sleep. Blinking as the room filled with a flash of light, I looked around, not sure if I was dreaming or awake. Creeping out of bed, I found myself standing by Dixie's window, peeking between the neon yellow curtains. Squinting, I could see the home next door and the main street, along with a few houses across the street.

The clouds above were black and rolling fast, bubbling like black boiling oil in the sky. I waited for the lighting show to start back up again... but it didn't; instead there was something else, circling above the house next to us, in and out of the black clouds. Wrinkling my nose, I squinted harder, trying to focus in the darkness. A glimpse of moonlight cast a soft glow on the earth. A huge black mass came over to the window and squatted on the ledge to look in.

I stood frozen, barely breathing. The jet-black skin was lightly covered in charcoal gray feathers. It had six eyes across its face in a line. It randomly blinked each of its eyes independently, turning them in all different directions. The mouth was human lips instead of a common bird's beak. Two penny-sized holes open and closed with flaps as it breathed.

Resuming my regular breathing, I determined this must be a dream. The creature extended its wings; underneath it had two arms on each side for a total of four. The eyes of the beast stopped moving in all directions and affixed on me only. Pursing my lips, I stopped breathing and remained still. *Did it see me?* I took a quick blink.

It opened its mouth, releasing an ear-piercing scream, exposing its pointed shark's teeth under the black lips. Millions of tiny birds flew out of its mouth and pummeled the window glass. My hands flew to shield my ears, holding them tight to protect them as best as I could. I doubled over, lost my balance, and fell towards the window, almost hitting my forehead against the glass.

Jerking myself backwards, I fell onto the plush carpeted floor. In all the commotion, I could see my backpack out of the corner of my eye glowing blue again. I focused on the mini raindrop birds pelting the window, resembling a downpour on a tin roof. The creature pushed off the ledge and flew into the sky as a blue light trailed behind him. I scrambled up, squishing my face on the glass to see where it went.

Believing this was just a dream, I crawled back into bed. The sound of the frame creaked as I turned around to get settled and try to put the dream out of my mind.

In the morning, Mr. Paul was already gone. Ms. DeeDee made us shrimp and grits for breakfast. Like most people in this area, she was an amazing cook. Once we finished cleaning up the dishes, I went to grab my stuff as Dixie followed me to her room.

"I have to tell you something," I told her.

"Oh no, I don't want to hear anything else."

"Don't worry, it doesn't directly affect you. I don't think I am going to enroll in college this semester."

"Does your mama know about this?"

"Not exactly."

"She is going to be so pissed at you!"

"I know, but if she doesn't come back home and I just forget to enroll... Well, shit happens!"

"Arielle, do what you want, but you need to find your path."

"That is exactly what I am trying to do, and school isn't going to help me right now. I need someone to help guide me with all the new stuff unfolding in my life. I feel so lost."

"I wish I could help, I really do. I don't know anyone in our circle that is willing to even talk about all the crazy things you have seen and deal with on a daily basis."

"I know. I can't think of anyone either. So many people shame me into not talking about the spirits. I am glad I can talk to you in private. At least you won't turn on me!"

She gave me a quick hug, because she knew I wasn't a very mushy person, and told me, "Come hang out again soon before school starts." I knew how crazy her schedule was going to be. She was on a mission to not just pass each class, but to knock it out of the park with all A's. She could do it, too, she was very smart. I put my hand on her arm and gave her a genuine smile. She smiled back. It's great when you find a friend who knows what you mean without having to speak a ton of words to verbalize everything you want to say to them. I started out of her room to head home.

"Oh," Dixie remembered, "Didn't you want to show me that book your papa left for you?"

"Yes!" Sitting on the floor of her room, I pulled the box out of my backpack and set the box gently on the floor and opened it. "What the heck?"

"What is it, Arielle?" Dixie rushed over to me and looked into the box, quickly turning to see my expression, "I thought you said there was a book in the box."

My face scrunched as I slammed the box shut and tossed it on her bed. "It was in here!"

"Did you check the box before you left your house?" she asked, reaching for the box and pulling out the hyssop oil. "What is this?" She turned the bottle and held it up to the light.

"I have no clue why that is still in here." I was angry I snatched it from her hand and stared at it. The bottle started to glow blue.

Dixie backed away. "Arielle, what the hell is going on? You are scaring me."

"You're scared? You are not living with this crap every day! With no real help from anyone. Forget it. It's not like you can really help me anyway." I stood up fast. "Look, I gotta go."

Dixie grabbed my arm as I was leaving the room, forcing me to stop and look at her, "There must be someone who can help you."

"When you figure that out, call me." Pulling away and throwing my arm up to get her to release me, I dashed out of her room, shoving the box and oil back into my backpack.

"Thank you, Ms. DeeDee, everything was lovely," I said, waving to her as I walked toward the front door and tried to be as chipper as possible.

"Make sure you register for your classes," she responded, not even looking up from her crossword puzzle.

Once outside, I pressed my helmet back on my head using both hands and securely clipping the chinstrap--all set to go. Placing my left hand on my handlebar grip, I swung my right leg over to mount the motorcycle, slamming my butt hard into the warm black leather seat.

Gritting my teeth, I gave the throttle a deep twist. As the bike roared down the street, I steered toward home. On the short ride home, I focused on taking deep breaths to calm down my anxiety. Nearing my house, I putted by the Old Ursuline Convent on the corner of Royal Street and Governor Nicholls Street. I slowed down, admiring the perfectly manicured green hedges, thinking to myself. *What am I going to do next? Maybe I should go for a walk and try clear my head?*

Standing in our courtyard next to the bike, I stared up at the house. With all the history in our house, I tended to feel very stifled and confined inside. Being Yankees, Mama and Papa didn't know much of the history of the city when they moved to Louisiana and purchased their home. They didn't know how haunted this house was, nor did they know the history of the previous owners. All they knew was that it was a great price and location in the middle of the city. Mama planned on having many children, and this house had a lot of rooms to fill.

Mark, my older brother, was born before they made the move to New Orleans. Mama wanted many more children, but God had other plans for their lives. After I was born, the doctor told Mama there were some complications and she would never bear any more children. Instead of being grief-stricken, she turned to her faith and prayed for God to give her more children.

Later that year, around Christmas time, there stood a woman at the front of the church explaining to the congregation about a new program in the foster care system. Mama slowly absorbed all Sister Peggy said as if she was only speaking to her. God gave Mama her open window for more children. Papa watched what was unfolding in front of him. Smiling at Mama, he scooped us up in his arms, releasing her to pounce on Sister Peggy with her questions.

"What are the first steps to make this happen for our family?"

Sister Peggy answered, "It is a simple process with a few home visits and a background check."

"I will be in your office on Monday to start all the paperwork." Mama beamed.

Before we rung in the New Year, Mama had several beds delivered. The first set of children were orphaned twins' brother and sister immigrants from France, Nicolas and Claire Benoit, age 17. Their parents left them alone in their New Orleans home while they had many family matters to tend to back in France. They wanted to have their children stay in the land of opportunities. Their plan to join their children the following year didn't transpire. Their ship was looted by pirates and there were no survivors. It sounds like something out of an old storybook, however pirates were still around plundering in the seas! At the age of 18, they both moved back to France to be closer to their other family members.

The first few sets of the kids were also Catholic making it was an easy transition for them to blend in our family. Mama Kaye and Papa Denny were learning the history of the city and making a new life for their little family, which was evolving into a big family.

The hauntings at our home didn't bother anyone directly, but me. Papa and Mama met with the priest after my constant protests over the years. The priest told them, "I will come by and see what is going on in your home."

Papa thanked him, "We look forward to your opinion."

"I have a few homes I visit about every six months and bless with holy water to help with the spirit activity." After his visit he told them, "Most of the hauntings were of children that used to live in the house. They wanted to be set free." The priest continued, "I did some research on the previous owners. They were from the early 1800's a doctor and his wife. They were exploratory people and had many slave children they purchased to "practice" on them to better their knowledge of medicine and science. The community didn't know these things were going on in the home."

Mama replied, "How awful! How could anyone do such a thing to innocent children?"

He continued, "From what I could find out, one of the rooms had a window that was bricked in no one knew they were doing awful things to these enslaved children. One of the slaves escaped and told the authorities. They didn't believe her, but visited the home and inspected it. When they came upon the room, the smell of burnt flesh and the moans of despair crept out of the cracks in the door." Mama buried her face in Papa's neck, trying to hold back her tears. "The wife and her husband fled the home and returned to Europe permanently, so the newspapers had reported."

There were many stories of the homes in New Orleans similar to this one. Growing up here, I believed all of them. I do think some have been embellished a little, but the core of the stories was true. And the lingering spirits here try to let their stories be known as a truth and not just some tale.

Often you can hear the tour guides talk about our home and point out the bricked-in window. When we were kids, at Halloween there was a lot more activity in the home and people passing by on the street. To enhance their experience, my brother and his friends would try to scare the tourists by throwing water balloons filled with red food dye in them. Mama did not find this funny one bit and their jokes were put to a quick stop.

Standing in the foyer I heard the house creaked and faint children's footsteps sounded going up the staircase. Nothing changed and I didn't want to hear any of it. I tossed my helmet in the closet, turned right around walking out onto the street to wander the city. My soul was so lost.

CHAPTER FIVE

Finding Friends

Keeping my head down, I studied the sidewalk and just kept walking, wracking my brain of where I could possibly go for help. Suddenly my body was engulfed in excruciating pain; I dropped to my knees; I couldn't walk. The agony started in my feet, numbing them. The numbing fire feeling crept up my legs as I became paralyzed. I grasped the air for help, but there was nothing to hold onto.

In the middle of the sidewalk on my knees, I reached towards the sky and cried out, "Speak to me. Tell me what's going on!"

If spirits were trying to get my attention. They sure had it! The pain started to diminish as it poured down my legs and out of my feet all the way to my toes. Breathing deeply, I was able to prop myself up, then gingerly rose to my feet. A few electric shocks of pain lingered.

Leaning forward with my hands on my knees, I took a few deeper breaths before I stood up completely. Once I had myself completely composed, my eyes lifted to greet Miranda right in front of me. We were so close I could see her eyes glistening under her black veil. Her cocoa skin was so smooth with high cheekbones and a delicate nose; she was a very beautiful woman. I've never been face-to-face with her before. She always seemed to vanish before I could really look at her. She loomed about five inches taller than me. The smell of roses and patchouli floated under my nose. I don't know why, but I tried to reach out to grab her veil from her face, but her hands snapped to my wrists and grabbed on tight. Unaware that I had another free hand, I froze in fear.

"You better watch yourself, girl," she hissed at me.

I stuttered back at her, trying to find the strength to say something clever, but all I could muster was, "Oh yeah, well... well... you better watch yourself, ma'am."

A high, shrill cackle rang out from Miranda. I felt like such a fool. Miranda continued, "In time, and I will steal what I want from you."

"What do you want from me?" I squeaked in a high voice.

"Soon enough you will see," And with that, Miranda released my wrist, flinging it high. I stumbled away from her. Her hands joined together at her palms as a blast of air shot at me. The cold air forced my legs out in front of me, causing me to slide butt first onto the ground. The uneven bricks ground into my tender elbows. Before I could even sit up, she evaporated.

Damn that woman! I yelled in my head. *I really wish she would leave me the hell alone!*

A disgusted sigh escaped my lips as I remained on my butt trying to peek at my elbow and inspect the damage. I looked up to see who was casting a partial shadow over me. All I could see was an arm extended, offering their hand to me. Placing my hand to my forehead to block some of the glare from the sun, a small smile formed across my face.
"Hi, Arielle. What are you doing down there?"

"Oh hi, Charlie, long time no see! Oh, ya know, just hanging out down here." I accepted his help and he softly pulled me to my feet.

He gently took my arm and inspected my elbows. "You are bleeding. Let's get you home and cleaned up." Guiding me back towards my home, I could feel the warmth of his hand resting on the small of my back.

Walking the short distance down the street, we turned towards my home. *Did he see what happened to me?* Finding courage, I asked, "Charlie, did you see exactly what happened to me back there?"

"Yes, you fell." Pausing for a moment, he stopped and turned to look at me. "But it looked like you were pushed. I didn't see anyone with you so that doesn't make any sense, does it?"

Turning and not wanting to show the concern in my eyes, I replied, "No, it doesn't make any sense at all." We were almost to the front door, so I tried to keep walking and slide my backpack off without touching my elbows. As the blood continued to dry on the scrapes, my elbows burned. Charlie noticed and he placed his hand on my shoulder to halt me.

He said, "Arielle, let me help you."

Allowing him to lift the backpack off my shoulder, I mumbled, "I really wish you could."

"What's that supposed to mean?"

I stuttered, "I--I--I'm sorry. I don't mean it the way you are taking it... I have so much going on and I don't know who to turn to." Pulling the backpack from him, he yanked it away from me.

"Arielle, whatever it is, I can help you." As he forced me to let go of the bag, our eyes met.

My gaze and my guard dropped as my voice scratched out, "I am just so scared, so tired, and I feel so alone right now."

Swinging the backpack on his back, he placed his hand on my shoulder and pulled me to him. I could hear the light thud of his heartbeat. "A hug can fix a multitude of things."

The warmth of his arms made me feel safe. A fleeting thought crossed my mind. *This could be another trap from Miranda!* Not wanting the moment to end, I closed my eyes and relaxed as much as I could. The sting of my elbows caused my eyes to flutter open.

Charlie broke the silence as he pulled back but still held onto my shoulders to view my face. "Come on, let's get you inside."

I patted under my eyes to wipe away any possible tears that escaped. He held me as I tugged on the zipper to retrieve the brass key with the small fleur-de-lis symbol stamped on the keychain. Opening the main door, we walked into the house. I hustled straight to the A/C thermostat and moved the small plastic level to cool the house off.

Charlie locked the front door and placed my pack in the kitchen. He followed me upstairs to the bathroom. Perched on the vanity, I dangled my feet as Charlie patted the wounds with peroxide. I tried to be a big girl and not whine from the white bubbles that formed along the scrapes. The cool breeze of his breath soothed the pain. Once the last Band-Aid was attached, my stomach let out a growl.

"Are you hungry or is that a tiger in your tank?"

I laughed and gave him a little playful push on his shoulder. I thought to myself, *Am I flirting?* This is unfamiliar territory to me.

"Let me take you out to lunch," Charlie suggested.

I glanced out the window. *It's early yet, but if we go out now it should still be light before we get home.*

"Hey, what is the problem?" he asked, waving his hand over my gaze to get me to look back at him.

How would I explain any of this to him? I liked Charlie and I didn't want him to think I was a crazy person. Bringing my vision back to him, I smiled and said, "No problem. Lunch sounds wonderful, but I should treat you, since you have been too helpful to me."

A sidewise smile crossed his face. "I'm an old-fashioned kind of guy. I should pay. Come on, let's go. But first..." Charlie pointed to my electric blue Cindi Lauper T-shirt.

"Oh no! No, my concert shirt!" Twisting I saw the tiny blood droplets on the sides. "I have to soak this before we go."

"Take your time. I wouldn't want to be the one blamed if your shirt didn't come clean."

As I ran cold water over the fabric, the brown liquid ran clear. I rummaged in the closet, deciding on the light pink shirt with a purple zigzag design running down the side. As we wandered the streets trying to decide where to eat, we chatted to pass the time. "I am in the Lake Borgne area near my cousin Nick. You should come visit me sometime. I would like to show you the area. Arielle, I definitely know about loss if you ever want to talk about your Papa. Maybe I could help."

Charlie was a friend of my brother's. They went to high school together at Brother Martin and we had some school dances together. I remember he had to move his senior year to live with his godfather, called in the Cajun world as his parrain. The summer before his senior year, his parents died in a deep-sea fishing accident. Neither their bodies nor the boat were recovered; not even the captain was found. You would think with such an event you would want to stay far away from the water, but he loved the simple living of the area and this became his new home on the lake. After his senior year, he lost his parrain to a heart attack.

"I may take you up on that sometime. But I don't feel like talking about it right now. Thank you for the offer though." Standing on Decatur Street, I pointed to a sign up ahead. "How about we eat at Frank's? I haven't been there in quite some time. This would give me time to talk about the rumors I heard about you! All of it sounds intriguing." He replied with a raised eyebrow.

Once we were both settled in a cozy red fabric booth, I opened the menu and pretended to look even though I knew exactly what I would order for dinner. "So, can I confirm the rumor about you and Nick running an alligator farm?"

"Yes, it is now confirmed. We have one of those places that schools load up the kids for field trips. The kiddos can see how the baby gators hatch from the eggs. And the most exciting part, see a few grown men wrestle with the ten-foot alligators!" Dropping his menu, he raised both arms, popping his muscles alternately.

"Only in the south. How does this all seem so normal to us down here? My Yankee family doesn't see the joy in such things. Maybe one day there will be a TV show about all this craziness." Fluttering my hand at him, still flexing, I ordered the crawfish Gagliano, a delightfully fattening dish with a garlic butter sauce. Charlie ordered the chicken marsala. Leaning back in the booth, I instinctively rested my hand on my belly. The waitress asked if we wanted dessert. "There is no way I could eat another bite. Unless you want dessert to go?" I asked, pumping my eyebrows at Charlie. "Would you like to come back to my house for coffee and dessert later?"

"That sounds great to me. Do you like Bananas Foster or bread pudding?"

"Oh man, I have to choose?" I asked dramatically placing the back of my hand across my forehead.

"We will take one of each to go."

Charlie was holding the two Styrofoam containers as we meandered quietly though the streets. The heat was thick on our short walk back. I envisioned the containers melting in his palms. Opening the door, a refreshing coolness greeted us from inside the house.

Peeking out the front door as I pushed it closed, I smiled at the sun starting to drop. We made home before nightfall! Moving around the kitchen like I knew what I was doing, I started the coffee,
44

and the silver pot started brewing. I placed the matching navy-blue coffee mugs with tiny white flowers covering them on the counter. I eased into the chair across from Charlie at the small bistro table in the kitchen. He broke the silence and pressed me with questions, "Are you ever going to tell me what is going on with you? What are you afraid of? I am not going to judge you!"

Breathing deeply, I just let go, "I have no one to talk to. No one who understands what is going on with me. Something has happened that is supernatural, and I don't know exactly what is happening either."

He didn't move a muscle, just calmly sat with his hands folded listening.

"The fear I have is indescribable. What you witnessed was an encounter... I did not fall; I was pushed!"

A half smile started to appear across his face.

My eyebrows furrowed and the coffee pot started a sequence of beeps to tell me it was done. I slapped my hand on the table as I hopped down from the chair. Pouring our coffee, I ranted, "Great, you don't believe me and now you are going to make fun of me with that smirk?" I was so busy fuming I didn't realize he was standing next to me. I jumped and spilled one of the cups of coffee. He quickly snatched up the kitchen towel and wiped up the spill.

He put his hand over mine. I became quiet and held my breath. He gently guided me to sit at the table, "Arielle, I am sorry but I don't think I am the right person to help you."

Pushing out the air I was holding in creating a sigh, then, feeling defeated, I said, "I really didn't think you could anyway." My head fell into my palms as I rubbed my eyes, wondering why wouldn't God send me someone to help guide me?

He finished making our cups of coffee and getting plates out for the dessert. With a light clink, he placed the coffee between my resting elbows. The aroma of the coffee filled my nose. "Maybe I can't, but I know someone who can." He whispered assuring me.

My eyes widened as I picked up my head to rest in my palms to look at him as he walked back to the counter for the dessert. A bit of fear left my heart thinking of the possibilities. "You are not screwing with me, are you?"

"No, I am not a turd like your brother." That lightened me up and made me laugh as well as he continued, "My Aunt Nina is familiar with a lot of these types of things. Arielle, you really shouldn't be messing around with stuff you don't know about. It really can be dangerous!" He sat across from me with the desserts arranged on one plate with two forks between us.

"I know. I am so lost and am getting scared." Looking over his broad shoulder I could see streaks of rain hitting on the window in the kitchen. The sun was gone, and thunder started to roll outside. "Charlie, you should stay the night in Mark's room, and you can go home tomorrow."

He agreed with a nod. "That might not be a bad idea with the weather getting nasty out there." He glanced over his shoulder to the window.

"Why are you in town anyway?" I asked.

"I had some items that I need to pick up from the hardware store to get things in order before the tours begin at the alligator farm next season." He smiled. "And as luck would have it, I ran into you."

"I don't believe in luck," I said, stabbing a piece of banana.

"Loosen up, Arielle."

"I wish I could. I am always on edge! Maybe after I meet with your aunt, I won't be so cynical?" I said with a frown.
46

I settled in my bed that night with less fear and a bit of hope. I was happy that Charlie was here and had thought about me meeting his aunt.

The dreams started to creep into my head like a black fog. I was alone, walking in the evening. I didn't recognize the area I was in, but seemed to know where I was walking to. The buildings were growing taller as I walked down the street. The windows extended high as the lights became dim. I felt like the street was shrinking as the building turned dark and loomed over me.

Jet black water began to pour into the streets out of doors and windows. Before I realized, the water was over my ankles. I pulled up my tan lace skirt to keep it from the water and walked quickly down the street. The buildings became all connected; there were no longer any side streets.

I couldn't find a way out; the water rose up to my knees. Fear crept in. *What could be in the water and how am I to escape?* I felt something grab at my ankle, and I screamed while being pulled under the water. Thrashing around, I came up to the surface and cried out for help. Under the water again, I could feel someone's nails scratching at my legs and ankles, trying to hold me down. I kicked as hard as I could and came up for a breath of air. *Someone to help me!* I shouted. My legs frantically kicked and were freed at last from the pull from the unknown creature.

"Arielle, Arielle!" My eyes rolled around in my head. Slitting my eyes open caused the dream to slip away from my mind. Charlie comes into focus, "Wake up, Arielle, are you okay?" he asked in a higher octave than his normal voice.

Unable to speak, I nodded *yes,* and closed my eyes tight. Charlie sat on the edge of my bed and waited for me to find my words.

"I am all right," I finally said. "What time is it?" I placed my hand over my ankle to feel the welt growing. I pulled back the covers to examine the damage.

Charlie glanced at the glowing clock. "It is 3 a.m.," he told me.

He rose to turn the overhead light on. "What the hell is that? When did this happen?"

I slowly shook my head. "This usually doesn't happen in my dreams. There are creatures trying to harm me but, they never left an actual mark before."

He took my hands and said a prayer for me. "Dear God, please watch over Arielle and keep her safe." He sat with me until I fell back asleep but not for long. I was actually up first so I made a great pot of coffee and crappy instant oatmeal. Apologizing to him, I said, "I really don't have much in the house to make a real breakfast. Sorry about that."

"I really don't care as long as the coffee is good. When are you coming to visit me?" Charlie asked after I picked up the dishes.

"I will come today... tomorrow at the latest, I promise. I really want to meet your aunt. I must do something. As you can tell, things are getting worse."

He jotted his number down on a cat-shaped notepad that was next to the kitchen phone. "Call me when you are ready, and I will meet you because it is tricky to find the place. I am going to run my errands and bring the stuff back to my camp. We usually meet the busses at the dock and charter the kids to the alligator farm."

"You can always meet me at my parents' camp and I can follow you to your place. It probably isn't too far away from where your camp is located. Right?"

"Yep, that's fine, whatever you want to do. Are you sure you are going to be all right alone?" He gave me a squeeze on my arm.

"Honestly as comforting as it is to have someone physically here, these things are going to keep happening no matter who is with me."

"That is very true." Turning back on his way out the side courtyard door, he said, "Make sure you bring anything that you think might be of help to you. Or anything you want to share with Aunt Nina."

"Okay, I will wrack my brain to see what I should bring with me." Peeking out the side window I watched him till he was out of sight. Stepping out into the courtyard, I sat on the bench to collect myself. A smile filled my face. Excitement filled my heart and replaced the fear that had been living there. *I am going to get some real help finally!* I started a mental checklist of everything I should pack for my little trip, like marshmallows!

CHAPTER SIX

Swamped

Walking through the house, I thought about all the things that had happened here. It creeps me out, especially when I am all alone. The hairs stood up on my arms and neck as a cold breeze funneled through, rattling the paintings on the walls and spreading paperwork throughout the house. As quickly as it started, it ended.

Standing in the kitchen, I made the list in my head I needed some things in my room and some here. Dropping the backpack on my bed, I turned on the light in the closet by pulling on the brass chain. I grabbed my boots and a few outfits and stuffed them into the bag. I pulled the box out of the closet that Papa left me and took out the hyssop oil and an extra boogieman spray. I slammed the box shut; I couldn't believe that book was still missing. But I really had no clue where to start looking for it.

Retrieving the batman flashlight from my nightstand, I flicked it on and shined a big bat symbol into the wall. *I hope that really helps me out if I need it. At least it is a bright light, as silly as it looks.*

I made my way downstairs for the rest of the items, making sure to turn the lights off as I went. The sounds from the attic stirred. I rolled my eyes with annoyance. Quickening the pace, I made it to the bottom of the stairs and rounded the door to the kitchen. Mama was a nut about s'mores, so we were bound to have marshmallows somewhere in here. Score! In the cabinet, there was an unopened bag. I maneuvered the plastic Abita bottles of waters in the bottom of the bag with the marshmallow on top so they wouldn't get squished.

Tapping my lips with my index finger, I wondered, *Did Papa have any maps of the waterways to bring just in case? Where would I even look for them?* There was a shop on Prytania Street that sold maps. I had been on the pirogue with Papa many times, but never alone so I never really paid attention to the routes. I didn't need a map since Charlie was meeting me. *Be smart, Arielle, get the maps.* A voice whispered in my head. Finally, I was being helped by my spirit guides. I needed to do my part and be smart. I swung the pack on my back stumbling a little from the weight and adjusted the straps, to keep it snug on my back, but long enough to sit on the seat behind me while I rode the motorcycle. Searching for my new helmet, I heard the noise upstairs again. I planned to leave out the courtyard door where I had parked the motorcycle the other day.

Real footsteps crossed the hallway above me. *Crap!* I thought to myself. That was not a normal spirit sound. I started to scramble around for my new helmet; maybe it was in the nearby closet. *Oh excellent, my jacket is in here!* That would be good to take for mosquitoes in the evenings.

A beam of light shined from the window. I followed the rays, and a glitter pink ball glistened. Yes, my *helmet!* I grabbed it and bolted for the side door. I gently closed the door, but it still creaked. I didn't even bother to lock the door. I quickly slapped my helmet on, mashing down my hair, and clipped the clasp under my chin. I swung my leg up high over the long seat, sliding onto the warm black leather.

Patting my pockets, I thought, *Where is the key? Ugh, in the outside pocket of my backpack.*

Sliding out of my backpack, I hopped off the bike. Finally, with the key in my hand, the courtyard house door opened. My heart sank; my eyes widened in fear as I gulped and stood frozen.

A figure ducked as it walked out into my full view. "Mark! What in God's green earth are you doing here?" I gasped, holding the key clenched in my right hand pressing over my heart. "Are you trying to give me a heart attack?"

A smug smile grew on his face, "You didn't answer the phone the last few times I called and you didn't call back from the messages I left."

"And, why were you in the attic?"

"Looking for Papa's old fishing gear. I thought maybe it was in the attic. Mom hasn't heard from you either, ya know. She called, asking me to check on you."

"I was home last night, and she didn't call me. I was going to call her this morning." I nodded to convince us both. "When did you get in the house anyway? How long have you been here?"

"Oh, not long, I came in through the front door. I saw you in the courtyard with Charlie."

"Oh... You saw that Charlie was here?" Not making eye contact I fiddled with taking my helmet off to place it on the handlebars.

"Yes." Standing tall with arms crossed, he tapped his foot loud enough to create an echo in the courtyard.

"Dammit, Mark, you scared the crap out of me. If you are looking for the fishing gear it is probably at the camp anyway," I growled at him.

"Why don't we go inside, and you can explain yourself and call Mama."

"Oooooh yeah, I really was going to call her before I left to tell her I was going to spend some time at a friend's house for a few days. But all that noise made me leave quicker than I anticipated." I pumped my index finger towards the roof line of the house.

"Where are you off to now?"

"I was at Dixie's for a few nights." I glanced around and played with the straps on the backpack as I lugged it back over my shoulders.

"Yeah... got that... but I asked where you are heading... *not* where have you been. Spill it."

"Um... I am going to visit Charlie for a bit." A little pink filled my cheeks.

Mark raised an eyebrow with one eye squinted. He pulled his head back a little, as if to process what I had just said to him. "Charlie is my friend. What exactly is going on between you two?"

I never had an overly mushy relationship with my brother. A quick pop with a fist in an arm would be a common greeting between us. Most people didn't understand our relationship, but it worked. Mark always looked out for me. No matter what other sibling, foster kids, orphans lived in the house, we were solid in having each other's backs, always!

Mama had a good heart and gave everyone the benefit of the doubt, especially kids. There were a few strays that lived with us that were beyond help. One in particular should not have been allowed to live in our home, Scott Anderson. He would mess with all the other strays, but he was always so cordial to Mama, Papa and Mark. Pulling the girls' hair and shoving the boys into the walls, Scott was a jerk. As a sophomore in high school Mark was 6'5". No one even thought about trying to bully him.

I liked to spend the evening, after the chores were done, in the courtyard until Scott started to sit next to me on the bench. He placed his arm around me and grabbed my shoulder, yanking me closer to him. I faced forward and didn't turn towards him. He grabbed my cheeks as he tried to lick my neck as I pulled away. Neither of us knew, but Mark happened to be on the upstairs balcony, secretly smoking a cigarette. He watched the event right in front of him. Slapping at him, I wrestled away from Scott's grasp and darted straight into the downstairs bathroom. His creepy cackle echoed after me. I splashed my face with cold water, trying to cool my anger. *Do I try to tell Mark, or my parents? Nothing really happened. He was just being pushy.* He was gone by the next morning. I never saw him around town again either.

After that our sibling relationship became even closer. I punched him as a thank you with a smile when I figured out what had happened. He patted the top of my head, nodding. Years later, he was still trying to look after me. He had his own family and farm to care for, a strikingly beautiful wife, Nicole, with the most infectious smile, their copper-top six-year-old son Eli, and acres of land with animals.

"I will go inside and call Mama before I leave."

"Good." He pointed to the door and followed me back into the kitchen.

"Hi, Mama, before you start in on me, I know, I didn't call sooner and you are mad, and yes, I'm fine. I'm eating, I'm sleeping, I'm getting my class schedule ready. I will call you in a few days. Did I cover everything?" I asked, pushing my tongue out at Mark who hovered in the kitchen.

"Thank you for finally calling. I love you, Arielle, and I miss you. I need to hear your voice!" she responded, "I will be coming home in about two weeks. Did you get a chance to look at that book Papa left you?"

"No. I wasn't able to open the book yet." I didn't want to tell her the damn book was missing, "I love you too, Mama, and I miss you a lot. Two more weeks?"

"Yes, around two weeks."

"Okay, well, Mark is here so let me go and I will talk to you soon."

"Tell Mark to call me when he gets home."

"Will do. Bye, Mama." I hung up the phone, watching Mark leaning against the counter sipping on drink. I grabbed it from him and took a quick gulp of the Tang drink, slapping the plastic Mardi Gras cup on the counter a little too hard causing the orange sticky drink to splash up onto my hand.

He didn't even flinch. "Why didn't you tell Mama you are going to see Charlie?"

I glared at him before running my hand under the warm water. "Seriously?" I asked him, flicking water across the kitchen towards his face. We both knew she would be on the next flight down here if I told her I was going to visit a boy. My back started to ache a little from the backpack that was still on. I adjusted the straps and shifted the weight around.

Mark lifted the pack up from the top loop, feeling the whole load, releasing it and caused me to stumble a little. "Looks like you are going to be away from home for more than just a couple of days."

Rolling my eyes, I said, "I will call you in a few days." Flashing a big smile, I eased towards the door, "Can you lock up here when you leave?"

Nodding, he fluttered his hand sending me on my way.

With the courtyard gate open, I rolled the bike, pausing for a moment to look for traffic. Leaning to the left the wheels bounced off the curb onto the street as I headed toward the map shop.

The little brass bell announced my arrival into the old shop; smells of old musty paper instantly filled my nose. I heard a muffled, "Hello, I will be right with you." It was a man's voice calling from the back of the shop.

"Okay, thank you!" Casually flipping through a local book on display of the New Orleans monuments, he emerged from the back of the shop. His wild white hair needed a trim, along with the matching hairs curling out of his nostrils resembling a hermit crab's legs. Trying to contain my amusement, I stated, "Hi, I need a current map of the Lake Borgne water channels please."

He held up one finger and shuffled away from me. He returned rolling out a map stretched onto the counter for me to view it; forcing the corners to stay flat he used large oyster shells for paperweights. Taking a minute to study it, my finger traced landing on our camp, tapping the location twice. The cash register rang out a cha-ching sound as the man said, "That will be four dollars and seventy-five cents."

"Perfect. Thanks." I handed him a five-dollar bill. "Keep the change."

He flipped the coin up into the air high, catching it with his right hand and his left thumb flung high thumbs up along with a quick wink.

With the map rolled up in the backpack, I had one more place to stop. I needed a sandwich from Maspero's on Decatur. A girl's gotta eat! Parking the motorcycle on the sidewalk, I breezed in and out. Examining my muffuletta, I could see where the grease from the cheese and olive salad stained the brown paper wrapper.

The plastic water bottle crinkled as I drank it fast to make room in the backpack for the sandwich. I gently placed the sandwich in the backpack, thinking *I will enjoy this when I get to the camp.* I tossed the empty water bottle in the nearby trash can and swung my leg high over the waiting motorcycle. "Hey, you can't park there!" The clip-clop grew louder, and I stretched to look over my shoulder to see a police officer on horseback approaching.

"Yes sir, I am moving right away." The engine was already purring. I rolled out, peeking at the gauge instruments. I didn't have much gas left in the tank. Papa always filled up the cars and bikes with gas, but this was something that Mama and I quickly learned to do. Did I mention I was blond? Sometimes I could be a real ding-dong. My brother used to say I had blond moments all the time. He also loved to tell me blond jokes as well. I wasn't dumb, I was just living in my own little world, not noticing things happening around me. I could hear Papa lecturing me already, that I needed to learn to pay attention for my own safety!

CHAPTER SEVEN

Stolen Book

I eased the motorcycle up into the small gas station on North Rampart Street and popped the cap in the open position the gas tank. 'Prepay' in bright red letters flashed on the pump as soon as I picked up the pump lever. I placed nozzle back and the cap on the bike, but didn't click it back closed. I hustled with the heavy backpack on to pay $5.00. *That should be plenty.*

I still didn't notice anything unusual around me as I pumped the gas and placed the nozzle back on the carrier. I didn't use the full $5.00, but didn't want to go back in and stand in line for 10 cents.

I was just about to put my helmet on my head when tightness crossed my chest and a cold flush of air rushed around my face. My head whipped around, scanning the parking lot. There were two very tall men stepping out of a black Lincoln car in dark suits. Fighting with the snap on my helmet, their pace quickened towards me. Unable to clip my helmet I tossed it in their direction. A loud crack sounded as it hit the ground.

I cranked the engine and tore out of the parking lot with the back end of the bike fishtailing. The men darted back to their idling car in hot pursuit. I have not ridden without a helmet before and was a little nervous about this, but more so about being in the hands of these men. I assumed they worked for Miranda. Wanting to lose them before heading in the direction of the camp, I planned an escape route in my head to weave in and out of traffic and take a side road to get out of their line of vision. I glanced back, trying to keep my balance with the heavy backpack on, and could see I was losing them. *Ha-ha, what a bunch of dufuses!*

Turning around to focus on the road, Miranda appeared on the sidewalk. Her arm extended, pointing her long black fingernail at me as I whizzed by. My cheeks remained flushed from the heat of the day, even though I felt my color draining from my face upon seeing her. She was really after me and she wasn't giving up anytime

58

soon either. I turned on another street, zipped up, and cut the next corner. There she was again! Her veil was up as her pitch-black eyes focused on me. I could see her ruby red lips curl around her white teeth. She was pointing again, but this time cradled in her left arm was my papa's book! How in the hell was all of this possible? There was no way I felt ready to confront her.

Leaning towards my side mirror, I saw that the men were now right behind me. I snapped my head up to look at the intersection. Miranda emerged directly in front of me. With no time to swerve, I locked up the brakes and slid on an angle towards her. I managed to keep the bike upright. Upon contact, her body swirled up into a smoky mist. As I passed through the mirage, her evil chuckle flooded my ears as her voice rang out, "Unlock the book for me or the gris-gris will engulf you."

The bike stopped as my left foot hit the ground. I was only a few blocks away from my turn onto Chef Menteur, leading me to our camp on the water. The illusion of Miranda slowed me down so much the men were revving upon me. Not wanting them to follow me to the camp, I peeled out back towards the city, trying to lose them in the jam-packed traffic.

The sounds of a brass band in the middle of the street forced me to slow down once again. The traditional slow brassy sounds of the funeral band echoed off the building around us. The people prepared for a second line funeral processional. The roads were not blocked off yet, but as the crowd gathered in the streets, they became their own roadblock. Veering the motorcycle onto a side road, I jerked back, realizing my mistake because it was a one-way.

Remaining seated, I walked the bike, weaving through the people to the next block, then cut to the left. Squeezing the handlebars, the bike squealed to a stop, just missing the car in front of me. The traffic was halted, as sounds of the brass band playing "Amazing Grace" on the next street rose over the buildings. Trying to wipe the hair out of my eyes that was plastered to my forehead with the mist of sweat forming, I glanced behind me.

Unbelievable, how did they make it through that crowd of people? There was one car between us. My left foot still on the pavement for balance, I twisted completely around. The sounds of an engine revving grew closer. These crazy guys lunged at the car between us, closer to me with each pump of the gas. Twisting the throttle, I pulled onto the sidewalk. The uneven brick sidewalks adorning the city made the ride terribly rough. It was hard to walk, even harder to ride on.

Luckily, the crowds of people were all on the next street for the funeral excitement. I bounced down the curb back onto the street ahead of all the traffic. The traffic cleared up ahead of me. *I lost them!* Studying the intersection coming up, a black car stopped in the middle of my path. The same men stood there with their arms crossed. *Am I ever going to get away from these goons?* I wheeled around, almost losing my balance on such a sharp turn.

Heading back towards the funeral I could hear the brass instruments ring out, "Oh when the Saints, go marching in." Colorful umbrellas adorned with decorations bounced up and down celebrating the passing of their friend or family member. They rejoiced in knowing they were going to Heaven. Whizzing by the funeral, I headed out of the French Quarter going north this time. *They are right on my tail again. This can't be real. How am I going to get away?*

I peered into the side mirror again to gage the distance, but they were gone. *Where are they?*

I crossed over into a different section of New Orleans now, out of the French Quarter. The men pulled their car in front of me and stopped again. A flashback to my motorcycle safety class taught me to jerk the handlebar to make a sharp turn around the back end of the Lincoln. I barely passed them. I turned my head to focus on them in slow motion. Their stark white skulls with hollow black eye sockets watched me pass by. They dissipated into smoke as evil laughter surrounded me. The sounds faded as I zipped down the road towards my family camp.

My head was spinning from all the bizarreness. I was a little farther north than I had planned, so I needed to find a road heading south that would intersect with Chef Menteur Highway. I didn't want to get on the interstate. Realizing I still didn't have a helmet on, my hair whipped around as the winds started to pick up as I neared the water. Thinking ahead, I wondered, *I hope there is an extra helmet at the camp.*

After about twenty minutes my eyes burned, but I saw the bridge up ahead and gripped the handlebars so hard my fingers turned white. Changing my position, as if I were on a horse about to jump over a log, I bounced for about five seconds. Once across the old wooden bridge, I came up on my turn onto Marques Road. This camp was our family's "off the grid" home. No one was ever invited to this home except Mama, Papa, Mark, and me. The first two weeks before summer and last two weeks before the new group of strays came in, we stayed here to regroup and recharge. It was our quaint getaway--an unlisted phone number with the bare necessities. Papa had built a camp directly next to this one for Mark and his family to have their own little getaway too, as a wedding present.

The last hurricane practically destroyed all the camps in this area. We were in the process of rebuilding when Papa passed away. All the rooms were not furnished yet, but it was livable. Happy to be here, I parked the motorcycle under the raised home and pulled a blue tarp over it to keep it protected and hidden. Keys in hand, I opened the door. Stepping inside, I could smell the newness of the construction.

The temperature in the home was just as hot and humid as outside. Going straight to the window unit in the kitchen, I pressed the on button, and after about five beeps, the max cool was set in place. Sliding the backpack off my sweat-drenched back on the floor, I leaned in, placing my hands on either side of the unit, the cool air blasting my face. Raising my face to cool my neck, I looked out the window at Mark's camp next door, thinking, *How much our lives have changed since we lost Papa. I miss having him here to talk to.*

Once cooled off, I snapped on the kitchen radio. The music resonated to the low sounds of, "Sweet Dreams" from Eurythmics. I started singing along, a little off-key, *Sweet Dreams are made of this...* I hoped I would have sweet dreams tonight. When the house was being rebuilt, as a family we decided we didn't want any upgrades, other than the home being raised along with cement pilings. Even though this wasn't the same home, it still felt the same.

My stomach growled at me, *Sandwich time!* Pushing the lingering thoughts of the current events out of my mind, I opened the kitchen cabinets. The same pattern dishes were stacked as if the dumb hurricane never occurred. Smiling with comfort, I held the plate close to me and traced the blue flowers with my index finger. Mama was good. She found almost everything we lost--the same colors, patterns--and she put everything back together here. It took her awhile to find everything, but she did it.

Setting the plate at the small wooden table, I pulled out one of the four chairs out and sat down. Licking the leftover grease on my fingertips, I walked over to the window and pulled the curtain with the back of my hand to see the sun over the water getting ready to kiss. I love this time of day at the camp; the sun sets very quickly. I didn't want to miss it. At dusk the bayou turns blue and the warm breeze would push the mosquitoes away. Giving my hand a wipe on my jean shorts, I picked up the phone and dialed the number Mama gave to me before she left. She made me memorize it and quizzed me daily the week before she left town.

Standing on the wraparound porch, leaning on the railing I watched the glowing giant orange dip into the water. The cord from the hunter green phone was stretched to the max to be outside. The sounds of the swamp changed just as quickly as the sun set. The lapping of the water was drowned out by the sound of the late-night bugs chattering. Several pelicans silently glided by, making their way home for the night. They dipped down and let the tips of their wings drape in the water, creating a rippling effect.

The machine picked up, and I listened to Mama's voice: "When you hear the beep you know what to do."

"Hey, Mama. I just wanted to check in again and let you know I am at the camp now. I will call you in a few days. I love you. Bye." I put the phone on the receiver and placed it on the deck. I wrapped my arms tightly around my chest, closing my eyes as I inhaled, smelling the air. Rain was on the horizon.

If Miranda has no idea I am here, maybe I can just stay here forever? I thought. *No, God has something planned for you. I don't think hiding in the swamp is what he really wants.* I opened my eyes and the sun was gone; the moon was not quite here yet. Rising I put the phone on the kitchen table and locked myself in for the night. I unpacked my backpack and piddled around the camp a little before I settled into some old PJ's I found.

Leaning over the bed, I said my prayers. "Dear God, please send your angels to watch over me. Please speak to me and let me know what plans you have for me in this world. I know you have bestowed me with a gift. I want to do good works with it and don't know exactly how to do this. Help a sista out, God. Amen." Climbing into bed, sleep filled my head, as I waited for the visitors to come.

CHAPTER EIGHT
A Dog Named Breeze

The morning came fast with a great night's sleep. As I rummaged in the pantry I thought, *Please let there be coffee in this house! Here coffee, coffee, coffee...* I held up a container of Sanka instant coffee, wrinkling my nose, *impostor!* There must be some community coffee in here somewhere, or at least Folgers coffee. There was a Folgers coffee plant not too far from here. When the wind blew just right, I could smell burning smell of the beans roasting. Knowing I needed more than just a whiff of coffee to wake up, the instant black sawdust would suffice for now. When I was a little more awake, I could search with a clear head to find something. The microwave beeped at me to tell me my fake coffee was hot.

Setting down the empty mug, I ran my teeth over my tongue several times, trying to get the thin coat of coffee buildup off. I started a new search. *There should be some boxed food in here I can cook up. Ah ha!* I found a packet of grits that would work for breakfast. I stepped outside, holding my bowl of grits. The clouds left a misty curtain in the air, making my skin wet. Sitting on the porch with the bowl and second cup of fake coffee, I took time to center myself and listen for guidance. Everything was so silent. *Sigh. These dishes won't clean themselves.* After washing them, I gently put them back in the cabinet. I began digging a little deeper in the pantry for coffee and lunch ideas. Finding a good supply of snacks, I piled them on the kitchen table for later.

After making a real cup of coffee, I walked outside to watch the nature as an unusual line of fog rolled in. The fog was usually gone at this time of day because the sun burned it away. Placing the coffee mug down on the railing, I rubbed my eyes. The fog rolled fast towards me, and the thick wet air slapped me in the face. Reaching out for the rail, I couldn't see anything as I felt my mug and heard a muffled shatter on the ground below. In the next blink the fog vanished. Leaning over the railing, straight down I saw a white fluffy dog with muddy paws next to the destroyed mug. He was sitting there looking at me. *That is odd.* There aren't any other homes nearby our camp. *The fella needs a haircut,* I thought. I can't see his eyes clearly because the fur is falling over the top of his brown eyes. *Cute thing, wonder if he is really real?* I quickly grabbed a pack of animal crackers off the inside table and made my way to the outside sturdy salvaged cypress staircase.

The dog stood on all fours and cautiously watched me walk towards him. "You are a little bigger than I thought," I told him as I was now on his level and not looking down from a second story. I slowly put my hand out with a cracker on my fingertips. Tongue out, he stepped forward and gently took the cracker from me and swallowed it after one crunch. "I don't see a collar around your neck. Is it nestled under all that thick white fur?" I spoke softly to him. "You must have an owner the way you are acting. I am going to reach for your collar. Okay?" He sat and let me reach to find he did have a collar. No phone number, but his name was Breeze.

Looking up, I prayed, "All right, God, what are you telling me now? I don't have any dog food here. What am I doing to do with a dog?" After a few more crackers, Breeze followed me upstairs, watching me get a bowl and fill it with some cold water. Placing the bowl on the floor, I talked to Breeze, "That is refreshing, isn't it? With this heat it has to be about 80 degrees already. Can you believe that it isn't even 9 a.m. yet?" Breeze lapped up the water, leaving the bowl empty except for a few small puddles around the bowl. "I always wanted a dog, but not having a real yard, Mama and Papa settled on cats, fish, and hamsters. You seem like a well-mannered dog." He sat at my feet or followed me all day.

Taking the rest of the day to search my soul, I asked myself and God questions, *What is my purpose? How can I protect myself from Miranda?* After pacing around the rooms of the camp, I took Breeze's bowl and a glass of ice water to recline on the porch. Finding a good shaded spot with the wind blowing nicely, I pulled the sway-back Adirondack chair there to settle in. Lounging in the chair, Breeze placed his paw on my leg as images pulsed and quickly flooded my head like a slideshow. All the people over the years I had delivered messages to flashed. I could see their smiling and some tear-streaked faces. Lastly, I saw Papa's book levitating. The book flung open and the pages flipped wildly and slammed shut! My clouded eyesight of memories faded as Breeze continued to rest his paw on my leg. Focusing on him, I asked, "What was that?" As I dissected the visions, I continued to talk to him. "So, I am supposed to help others when I can't even help myself. How is that for ironic?" I asked Breeze, "I must be here to help people. That is obvious. I know I may not have all the answers for everyone, but I guess I can give them enough so they can cope and move on. Is that my only purpose? What about the book? How do I get that back?" This was a lot for a nineteen-year-old girl to digest. Breeze went out of focus as my eyes filled with tears. "I don't know if I have the strength to do this. I am scared. If I could hear Papa's voice again. He would know just what to say to make me feel strong," I sniffed.

"You got this, Elle, I am here with you," Papa's voice echoed in my head. I smiled slightly, loving to hear him call me by my nickname that only he used.

"I miss you so much. My heart aches to have a conversation with you, Papa."

"Watch out for Miranda," he echoed again.

I cupped my face with my hands. "I need someone here to help me, Papa. Send me someone who can help me!" I begged. I listened, but his voice was gone. Breeze nuzzled my leg with his head. I dropped my hands and my face met his. A smile came across his face as he started to pant a little and his paw was back on the cypress wooden floors no longer touching me. Placing my hands around his head, we leaned in to touching foreheads. He gave me a big lick on the nose to break the silence. "Yuck, Breeze! Don't lick me!" Laughing, I wiped my nose with the back of my hand.

Moving inside for the rest of the day to try to beat the sweltering heat, we found some canned tuna and had lunch together in the small kitchen. I began talking to Breeze like he was human and half expecting him to even answer me like Papa's voice on the porch, but he didn't, "Okay, Breeze, let's talk this out. From what I know about Miranda, she can cast spells with her voodoo powers." I started to count out all my points on my hand showing my hands to him. "Two, she is an evil person who conjures dark spirits for guidance. Three, I know she wants to take my powers, or gifts, whatever you want to call them. Now what do I do about it?" We sat in silence, staring at each other.

I opened the door to let Breeze back in and told him, "Tomorrow I will call Charlie so we can go on Papa's pirogue to his camp. Maybe his Aunt Nina can really help me. I pray that she can." I slept on the couch that night with Breeze curled up at my feet.

CHAPTER NINE

Gators Going To Get You

Sometimes my dreams feel so real... I heard thunder as the lightning came closer. The rain dropped from the deep clouds, splatting on my face as I looked up. Images started to appear as the lightning flashed. I saw creatures in the sky fighting. The thunder sounded when the creatures collided. Some had swords drawn to strike each other. Their bloodshed became the raindrops falling from the night sky. The lightning swirled as I looked beyond the bolts. I could see another world trapped behind an invisible wall with claws, arms, wings, and other unrecognizable things that I didn't understand.

They were trying to climb into our realm. The fight was fierce, but the protectors on our side kept the other evil demons out. I recall seeing a tiger with wings holding a double-edged sword. There were casualties, and the fallen ones burned up like fire as they fell from the sky like meteors. The tiger let out a roar that was louder than any thunder I had ever heard before. I was glad when the storm passed, and the battle ended.

Waking up confused, I realized where I was when I felt fur in my toes from Breeze. He crept up next to me and gave me a yawn and sneaked in a lick on my cheek. Stretching, I patted him on the head and pushed him gently from my face, so he wouldn't lick me twice.

"What a strange dream that was last night." I said to Breeze, practically inaudibly, as I yawned.

Once we had sat down for breakfast it dawned on me. I called to Breeze who was enjoying his grits, "Ugh! I left so fast I didn't get the phone number to call Charlie. Another lovely blond moment!"

Breeze let out a whine as he looked up at me with grits plastered on the tip of his black nose. I laughed at him saying, "How hard could it be to find his place? I mean there should be signs or something for the field trips to go there. Right?" I motioned to Breeze. "Come here so I can wipe your face clean!"

A light wind blew of the lake, softening the promised heat of the morning, as I made my way to the pirogue tied up at the dock under the camp. Placing my backpack in the pirogue, I dropped my sunglasses from the top of my head down to my eyes to cut the glare of the rising sun's reflection on the water. Pirogues are tricky vessels, balance is everything. Placing my feet flat on the boat's floor and leaning across I pushed off from the pier just as Breeze leaped off the dock, landing in the middle of the boat and rocking it a bit.

"So, I guess you are coming with me?"

He placed himself on the floor of the boat in the middle facing forward. Sitting behind him on the metal bench. I took in the purity of the swampland. I love the green leaves and the luster of color as the sunshine glistens through the trees. Being out here makes me feel so safe and free. I may have Yankee parents, but my blood is all Southern.

The smooth wooden oar dipped into the water. I maneuvered into the narrow waterway. Swirls of green algae moved as the bow of the pirogue parted the water, stagnant here since no one had passed through in quite a while. The mosquitoes began buzzing around my face. Our two camps were secluded. About five miles away there are some other homes so there isn't much activity here.

I began watching the dog and not the map that was still rolled up in my backpack. He would turn his head and I would go in the direction he faced. Letting him guide me through the swamps, I noticed the waterline on the cypress trees, the dark water stain on the base indicating a low tide--one of the many things I learned from Papa. An egret perched on a cypress knee, fishing for his meal as I glided by quietly. I respected the wildlife and didn't want to disturb natural balance. Steadily paddling for about an hour, I broke the silence as I whispered to Breeze, "What a beautiful day this is turning out to be. Hot, but beautiful."

He didn't even notice I spoke to him, so I kept on paddling. We must be making decent progress and getting closer to our destination. I followed Breeze's head that turned left, as we heard low croaking sounds. *Oh, crap where is my backpack? I need those damn marshmallows now!* Trying not to panic, I saw a set of eyes and nostrils in the water floating nearby. The dark water masked how deep the water was in this area. I extended the oar straight down in the water. It scraped against the rocks and debris, indicating it was about five feet deep. Starting to paddle harder, the alligator came up fast as he bumped into the boat rocking it.

"Crap! This is bad," I told Breeze.

I tossed about four marshmallows overboard and paddled faster. He gobbled them up, along with a second alligator that got one of the puffy white treats. They turned towards us and gaining quickly. I looked at Breeze as he looked at me and then focused to the right, I took the turn onto that waterway. The water looked as if it ended up ahead, but I had trusted him this far and I wasn't about to stop.

I tossed few more marshmallows overboard to slow them down. Coming into the opening from the waterway, I recognized where I was, Alligator Bend! Charlie lived somewhere close to here. I started to have a tight feeling in my chest of pure panic as the gators seem to come out of nowhere and circle around the pirogue. This would be why the area was called Alligator Bend. The river created a 90-degree turn and the gators hung out here. The fish slowed to maneuver in the bend to pass through, making an easy catch for the gators.

My voice cracked, "Breeze, I didn't really think this through all the way, did I? There are more gators than marshmallows and it seems to attract them towards me rather than distract them."

Oh man, that was a big one... he came slow and steady as I dropped the oars into the boat. He ran into the side of the pirogue. My knuckles turned white as I held on to both sides of the boat to steady ourselves. Breeze looked at me with his head cocked to the
70

side and one ear up, as if to say, 'Come on, let's row!' I grabbed the oars and started the pirogue moving again.

The gators were getting so dense I wasn't able to paddle without hitting one or two. This was going to piss them off for sure! I needed to get to the other side of the bend to look for Charlie's camp or anyone's camp.

"I don't think we are going to be able to pass," I called over the hissing and croaking sounds of the gators to Breeze. One of the gators grabbed hold of the oar, and with one chomp, he ripped the paddle out of my hands and took it under the water. Letting out a loud yelp, I looked in the direction the gator swam off in and saw the oar pop up to the surface about ten meters from me in two pieces. Yikes! *That is not a good thing.* I began yelling at the gator. My voice carried across the water, bouncing off the nearby trees with a little echo.

"Get the hell away from my boat!"

I turned my focus back to the front of the boat. I almost jumped out of my skin. Breeze was inches away from my face. I stared into his eyes, and a calming wave came over me. My shoulders relaxed as I breathed out deeply and closed my eyes.

I said a little prayer. "God, I could use a little help down here for me and my new dog and me to get us out of this mess."

The boat rocked again, and my eyes popped open. There before me was a swirling white mist evaporating, and Breeze was gone. I glanced looked over the side of the boat where a wide mouth with rows of white teeth and a pink tongue pushed up over the side of the boat. The hissing sound surrounded me, making my head swim as I became dizzy.

I raised the oar over my head to make contact with the gator. Kablam! The gator instantly dropped off the side of the boat.

Tossing my head in all directions, I recognized the sound of a gunshot and tried to locate it.

CHAPTER TEN

Swamp Life With Charlie

As I frantically scanned the area, an airboat glided around the bend. Charlie stood on his boat steering with one hand and shotgun in his other hand and resting the base of the gun on his hip. The gators dropped down in the waters and disappeared in the dark waters. A few eyes and nostrils were along the shoreline watching us.

Thank you, God! The airboat came up fast. Killing the roar of the fan, he swung around the side of me and came to a sudden stop. The wake from his boat caused mine to rock as I held onto the sides again and gave him a sheepish grin.

"Arielle, you were supposed to call me! Don't you remember that?" he asked with a crooked smile. At least he seemed happy to see me. My mouth opened to answer as he motioned with his gun. He started up the airboat and the fan blew my hair all around I could barely see.

He circled around to be behind my pirogue and hollered over the rumble of the fan, "Head to the left of the bend."

I paddled with the one oar, a little on the left and then switched to the right to keep me from going in a circle. Thoughts raced in my mind... *What was he thinking of me being here? Was my hair a mess? God, I hope I look cute paddling this boat. Wow, I am hungry. I hope he has something good for dinner.*

Once around the bend, I saw his dock and the modest camp that he lived in. He had a few varnished alligator heads mounted to the piling on the bulkhead. He parked his airboat and quickly tied up, then he came over to mine to steady the boat with his foot, giving me his hand to help me up onto the pier.

My already flushed face turned a little redder as I took his hand. He stood about a foot taller than me. His dark thick hair was a little long curling over the tops of his ears. After taking his coarse hand, our eyes met and locked for a brief moment. Charlie's eyes were crystal blue. I could see the reflection and movement of the water.

Quickly feeling awkward, I glanced away. Gently biting my lower lip, I pushed off the pirogue and grabbed both his arms.

In all my grace, I slipped; the boat went left and we both went down into the water. We popped up like corks. He shook his head to remove the water from his locks, flashing a smile. I am so embarrassed all I could do was shrug as we treaded water. Making our way to the short ladder, I climbed on the pier with Charlie right behind me.

Charlie gathered my things out of the pirogue as I called to him while I tried to shake off some excess swamp water. "Are you sure you don't want me to get back in there to collect my stuff? I might pull you into the water again?"

I could see him bouncing from laugher trying to contain the belly laugh he wanted to release. He handed me my backpack. Keeping the bag of marshmallows, he held them up to inspect the bag. "You know this is the worst thing to feed them; it is all empty calories!"

"Thank you." Taking my bag and snatching the marshmallows, I said, "Maybe they were for me?" As I stuffed a whole one in my mouth with a smirk. I followed him up the stairway to the raised camp.

"Sure, they are for you, okay, okay. I will put them on the table for you to enjoy later then." His hand curled up, motioning for me to follow him, "You can shower here. There are fresh towels in the cabinet," he said and pointed to the small hand-built box next to the sink. "I am going to use the outside shower to get cleaned up," he said closing the door and leaving me alone in the bathroom.

"I'm sorry about that back there," I called through the door.

"Arielle, it is okay. You make life more interesting. I don't mind," he said as he tapped twice on the door.

Taking my shoes off, I poured out the swamp water in the bottom of them into the shower drain. I guessed I was going barefoot because those were the only shoes I brought with me. My stomach let out a low growl thinking about the marshmallows. *Maybe I should have eaten some more.*

I scoped out the shower to see what products were in there, shampoo and a bar of soap. Charlie must not have many showering visitors. My hair was going to freak out with no conditioner, but this wasn't the Hotel Monteleone with the fancy bottles of shampoo and conditioner. Lathering my hair, I thought about my parents. Every year they would take off for a weekend at a hotel for their anniversary, bringing back the mini bottles, such a simple memory forever etched into my brain.

On a normal day I'm sure Charlie was not being pulled into the swamp. Trying to make my hair presentable by running my hand upward through the sides of my hair, it flowed straight down practically plastered flat against my head. My top right tooth nibbled on my bottom lip as my stomach flipped and my mind raced about being here. Changing my thoughts, my heart leaped thinking about meeting Aunt Nina tomorrow. Running my hands and trying to fluff it up, I took one more glance in the mirror, patting my lips and blowing a kiss to myself. *Good enough.*

Once refreshed and clean, I gathered my bag, but left my white Keds, with a hint of green coloring, in the bathroom upside down in the tub, hopeful they would drip dry for tomorrow morning. I paused in the hallway to look at the line of old photographs. I touched a honey-colored frame and straightened it, leaning in for a closer look. It appeared to be Charlie as a boy in blue overalls, no shirt, posing with a grin and a fishing pole.

I side-stepped to the next photo; two people stood there frozen in time smiling. Even though I felt comfortable with Charlie, my stomach fluttered thinking about being here. My tummy growled at me as the aroma flowed from the kitchen. I looked down, and I placed my hand on my tummy as it growled at me again. Grateful to have a home-cooked meal, my eyes teared a little, thinking how much I missed having Mama home over the summer. I tried to decipher the scent coming from the kitchen.

I moved down the row, glancing at each of the framed photos. It must be something Cajun from the spices that linger in the thick warm air. As I approached the kitchen door, I gently leaned on the frame, watching Charlie's back as he stirred something in a large black pot on the stovetop. The kitchen was so small he only had to lean a little to the right to peek into the oven to check on the bread without taking a single step. When the oven door opened, the wonderful distinct smell of fresh garlic French bread filled the room.

My stomach growled, and Charlie turned to glance over his shoulder at me. With a smile he asked, "You are not hungry, are you?"

"My tummy can't lie," I replied, rubbing my stomach in a circle motion and setting my backpack down on the kitchen floor next to the table.

"You are in luck. We are having jambalaya with alligator sausage."

"I am so ready to eat one of those alligators that were trying to eat me today! And for dessert, bread pudding?"

"Yes, those alligators get what they deserve. We will see about dessert, though, that bread didn't do anything to you like the alligators did," he joked.

At this point I would never admit to Charlie that I didn't really like jambalaya, but I think I could eat anything. He handed me a glass of sweet tea, motioning for me to have a seat at the small table with only a few mismatched chairs. Most of the camps nowadays didn't have a lot of space because they are more of a getaway than a permanent residence for most folks. Charlie's camp was a two-bedroom one-bathroom shack on stilts with a lot of history. Most of them had been in the family for more generations that you can count on your fingers. They had weathered many storms, hurricanes, and floods. Some had washed away and been rebuilt taller and studier with hurricane straps on the studs to reinforce anything Mother Nature would send their direction.

Turning the glass of iced tea in my hands, the condensation that formed on the outside soaked my palms. I studied them and decided the best place to dry them was on my acid-washed denim jeans shorts.

I looked up and Charlie was standing there, one oven mitt on and a side smirk on his face. "Dinner is ready if you can pull yourself away from your deep thoughts."

I hopped up, banging my knee on the underside of the table. My tea hopped once and landed safely back onto the table as I pressed my lips tight together, trying to keep the yelp inside.

"You going to survive your injury?"

I whimpered back, "Yep. I'm fine."

He handed me a plate and pointed with his oven mitt to the stovetop. Being very selective, I spooned the food on my plate. I liked the alligator sausage. I made sure to put a lot of it on my plate. He placed the garlic bread on the table. We sat down across from each other and he folded his hands. I followed his lead bowing my head, "Bless us, O Lord, and these Thy gifts which we are about to receive from Thy bounty, through Christ our Lord, Amen."

After I inhaled dinner, I leaned back in the chair and took a large stretch and a yawn, almost toppling over backwards. With my eyes wide after catching myself, I could see Charlie shaking his head and laughing lightly at me. "Did you enjoy your dinner?"

"Yep, so much I will even offer to do the dishes!"

"The dishes can wait," he said depositing our plates in the sink. He pressed the round black button, the basket slowly dripped, filling the glass pot with coffee. Now that our attention was taken off something pressing, like dinner, the silence hung in the air.

I gave him a sideward smile, saying, "Sooooo, who are in the photos in your hallway? It looks like a lot of history on that wall."

"They are all photos of the Chaisson family starting from the first generation all the way to me, Charlie Chaisson. The last photo is me, the one with the fishing pole. We were using the camp as a getaway, not a home at that time. And, you are right. There is a lot of history in this camp, just like yours, I am sure."

"Our history isn't dated back nearly as far as yours is, but lots of great memories have been made at our camp."

"Did y'all have to rebuild after the last massive storm?" he asked me.

"Yes, we had to really rebuild from the ground up, but we have the hurricane straps now and reinforced walls with pilings. I think we are good for anything else that might come our way."

"I did all those precautions right after I moved here with my uncle. This last storm only damaged a few windows. We were pretty lucky." Charlie leaned forward on the table, stood up, and brought the coffee back to the table. The clinking sounds of our spoons on the coffee cups echoed in the small kitchen area. Pausing after his first sip, Charlie asked, "Did you get your college classes scheduled for fall?"

Stirring, I glanced sideways at the ceiling. "Not exactly, I know what classes I want to take, but technically I have not signed up for any."

"If you are serious about college, you need to sign up before all the good classes are gone."

"I know. I have heard this speech from several people. I will do it when I get back in town." Changing the subject, I said, "When can I meet your aunt? I really would love some guidance with all this craziness."

"I wanted to take you on a little tour of the farm tomorrow if you would like? We can row over to see Aunt Nina the next day."

"That sounds like a lot of fun." I raised my cup in the air, Charlie raised his mug to meet mine with a dull clunk. With only a few gulps left, I finished up my coffee and placed it back onto the tan placemat in front of me.

"Sounds like we have a plan. But for now, get some rest. I will even let you sleep in if you want too."

I gave him a weak smile to agree. I was mentally and physically exhausted from... everything.

"Do you think you will be able to sleep after that cup of coffee?" he asked.

"That is the last thing I worry about when going to bed. I can fall asleep no problem. I worry about the bad dreams that creep in!"

"Well, let's pray for sweet dreams then."

"I love it. Yes, sweet dreams for everyone!" I exclaimed before I walked out of the kitchen. Turning abruptly around, I said, "Wait, I was going to do the dishes."

"Go to bed, Arielle." He pointed towards the hallway.

"Yes, sir." I said with a double thumb's up.

I dropped my bag on the floor next to the bed and didn't even change my clothes to my PJs. Flopping onto the guest bed, I fell in a deep sleep as soon as my head touched the soft light blue pillow. I didn't even think back on the day or even saying my nightly prayers. I was just too tired from all the events.

Normally I would pray for a good night's sleep, just like Charlie suggested. Regardless, I still had visitors in my dreams; some were good, and some were nightmares. The dreams flooded in full force tonight. I was walking in the swamps. I could feel a spider web drape across my face. Using my hand I swiped at it, trying to shake it off. It landed in my hair, on my arms, as spiders began to pop up out of the marsh surrounding me. I started to stomp to try to kill or scare them away. My feet only squished around in the soft mud. The ground turned black from the dense amount of spiders. They piled up over my feet trying to climb up my bare legs.

Wake up, Arielle it is just a dream! I shouted to myself. I sprang up with a shot in bed gasping, while still shaking my legs and patting them as if the spiders continued to crawl over me. I had gotten used to the scary and odd dreams, but the feeling of not being rested really bothered me. I can't remember when the dreams all began, but it affected my life. I was labeled a bad student because I was always tired from sleepless nights accompanied with bad dreams. I didn't fail any subjects, but I didn't make the honor roll either. Maybe that's part of why I procrastinated to sign up for classes? Or it could just be there was too much crap going on in my life. Maybe I really should take a semester off... I drifted back asleep and there were no more dreams the rest of the night.

My eyes started to flutter open as the smell of bacon filled my room, along with my favorite beverage brewing. The daylight started to creep in from the plaid curtains covering the small four-pane window. As I got my surroundings, I dragged myself out of bed.

Pressing my palm against my head, I thought, *Ugh. I need coffee stat!* I didn't even make it to the bathroom first, creeping down the hall to get a cup of sweet nectar of life to give me the ability to communicate with the world. Charlie was there in the kitchen again. I wondered if he even slept last night. He must have, because he was wearing different clothes. So, I figured he at least left the kitchen.

I shuffled over to the coffee pot as Charlie let out a snorting laugh, "Nice hair."

I just blinked at him over the rim of the coffee cup. The steam from the mug as I drank distorted my view of Charlie, I just closed my eyes. I had nothing clever to say this early in the morning anyway. He would learn, I am not a morning person. I shuffled away back to my room and to find my bag to get ready for the day.

*****

"Okay, pay close attention. We are going to see how an alligator kills its prey," he quickly continued when he saw my eyes growing in size. "Don't worry, there will be live animals injured in this show, I hope."

"Thank goodness--wait, what??" I said very breathy, not realizing I was holding my breath to see what was going to possibly get killed.

"It's okay, Arielle. It's just marshmallows."

Charlie proceeded create a croaking sound from this throat. Then several dozen sets of eyes popped up in the marshy water around the raised wooded porch. "Here we go!" he called out as he used his PVC pipe marshmallow gun to rocket the white puffy treats far into the water. With each plunk sound the marshmallows made an alligator glide over. With one fast hard chomp, it sank underwater, only leaving a ring of tiny bubbles. "Once they have their prey they go deep, to make sure they drown the marshmallow so it doesn't put up much of a fight."

"That is really creepy. You tell this to small children who come out on this field trip?"

81

"Of course, I do. These kids need to be educated on gators. But don't worry there is some fun stuff we will do too. I start with this to put fear in them so they don't do anything stupid."

"That actually makes very good sense. So, show me something else the kids really love."

"You got it, follow me." He motioned with his hand after placing the marshmallow gun back into the handmade wooden box nailed to the side of the porch. I skipped once to catch up to him. "We are going to the hatchery next. All the eggs have hatched. The babies come in mid-August, sometimes early September. But I can show you the area and where the mother gators nest and stuff like that. I also have some larger babies you can hold, if you would like to."

"I assume it is safe if you have kids holding alligators, right?"

"Don't worry, I would never put you or anyone in direct danger. I use electrical tape to wrap around their mouth just while you hold them to protect both parties."

"I can't decide if I want to hold one, maybe later... I would like to see the nests for sure." I followed behind him.

We entered a boarded-off area that appeared to be an enclosed pond. The middle of the pond had large marsh muddy areas. Along the perimeter, Charlie had built wooded slats that fully enclosed the area down into the water.

He pointed over the side. "That is the entrance area where the enclosure allows the mothers to come into this protected area to lay their eggs and we can observe them in this natural habitat. If the mothers don't want to come in and lay their eggs they don't have too. Since they have been laying eggs here for generations they keep coming back." I was still looking at the structure of the area when Charlie gently pulled my arm to keep me moving, "Over here you can see the muddy area where the eggs were laid last season."

"That is amazing they feel so comfortable they come back here to hatch their babies. You sure have a lot of knowledge about alligators, don't you?"

"Yeah, we are like a little family. Although they are wild reptiles, we have learned to respect each other and work together. Would you like to hold a gator?"

"I think I am okay. I don't feel that that is on my bucket list. Unless it is a purse, I think I would hold that," I joked with him and gave him a little punch on the arm. The rest of the day we spent on the porch watching the slow life of the swamp go by... chatting about our families and our dreams.

Charlie was not in the house when I rolled out of bed the next morning, finding my breakfast on the counter, I ate standing there and quickly washed my dish and put it on the drying rack. Dishwashers in the camp houses were your own two hands.

Ugh, he sure was an early riser. I guess having to be ready for the field trips to his camp for the alligator tours required long and early hours. Standing on my tippy toes, I peeked out the window. I could see Charlie at the bottom of the pier, getting things in order for our little trip to visit Aunt Nina. After I gathered my bag, I left it in the room all packed up. I tried not to over process the questions building in my head. They can take over causing me to be too nervous, upsetting my stomach.

Okay, Arielle, try to let life just happen. Don't stress, stop trying to plan everything out. Nothing really works out like I think it will when I try to devise a plan in my head anyway. *Just let the spirits guide you,* I told myself. *Charlie is here to help you. Let him do that. Don't let yourself get in the way!*

After my little pep talk, I felt ready for my newest adventure. Heading back to the kitchen, I chugged down the last bit of coffee. Giving the mug a wash, I placed it upside down next to my clean dish. I bounced out of the house, down to the pier. Charlie was there with a large-brimmed hat. I held up a finger and ran back up to the camp and grabbed my light denim baseball hat, slapping it on my head and meeting him back at the pier.

"Where are we headed?" I asked.

"Into the swamp," he said.

"I thought this was the swamp," I joked

"You haven't seen the swamp yet." He smirked.

CHAPTER ELEVEN

Finding Trust

Charlie steadied his piroque with one leg in the boat and one leg on the pier. Offering me his hand to help me into the vessel, he gave me a weary smile.

"I got this, don't worry," I said taking his hand. I was super glad I didn't tip us over this time. I sat in the middle section as he positioned himself in the back of the boat, and with a quick push we were on our way.

I wondered how long it would take to get there, but I kept the questions to myself and took in all the beauty of the swamp around me. The sun was not high in the sky yet. The calls of the birds sounded around us. No surprise, the glorious mosquitoes were out this early in the morning too. I gently slid off the seat to put my butt on the bottom of the boat, so I could lean back and rest my head on the bench, looking at the passing clouds. The white puffy clouds started to take shape and my imagination picked out animal shapes.

Charlie navigated the pirogue, peacefully paddling. The sounds changed, and the view of the clouds started to disappear by the overgrown cypress trees. An egret flew over us out of sight over the trees. I sat up looking around, not that I would know where we were located. The green algae, also known as duck weed, surrounded my boat the area had a musky smell. I wrinkled up my nose at the smell, pushing a long breath out to try to clear out the heavy stink. I even tried a little double cough to escape the smell; that didn't work either. The heat continued to climb. Taking off my hat, I fanned my face to try to cool down my head a little. At least there was shade around us now, but this also kept the breeze from blowing over the narrow waterway.

Charlie broke the silence, "We are getting close. I want to give you a warning. My Aunt Nina is a little different," he stated.

Carefully, I shifted on the seat and faced him, "Um, now you tell me a warning about your aunt? What do you mean by a little different?" I asked in a higher octave than normal.

Not answering, he focused on the waterways and began paddling. The area had become very dense. This must be what he meant by into the swamp. "I would like you to tell Aunt Nina your story." He shifted his eyes to mine and gave me a wink and a smile. "Don't worry."

As the trees loomed overhead, everything started closing in on me. I was going to have a panic attack. Trying to keep calm, I rocked my head and nodded in response, "Okay." As if telling Charlie okay and also telling myself everything was going to be okay.

"When we get there stay with the boat, I will come back and get you. She lives out here for a reason and doesn't have many visitors. I don't want to startle her."

"You didn't call her and tell her we were coming?"

"No, she doesn't have a phone."

I nodded again. My heart picked up a pace, not sure what to be expecting. *You trust Charlie so there is no reason to be nervous.* I told myself. I studied Charlie's face as we went down the waterway. His sun-tanned face and arms from working outside all the time was a huge contrast to my pasty white skin.

I glanced over the side of the boat. Seeing no more algae, I could see my reflection in the water since it was so dark and smooth off the side of the piroque. *Man, oh man, I need a haircut when I get back to town.* I was embarrassed to be meeting someone new looking like this, but it was too late now. Turning my focus ahead, I could see the water passage widening.

"Are we stopping...?" I asked.

Charlie landed the boat and tied us off before I even finished my question. "Yes, we are here."

He hopped out and walked up to the shack perched on tall stilts. He paused, turning back to give me a smile as if to say, *Don't freak out. Everything is okay.* I flashed a weak smile, showing my top teeth his way, and I looked down to study my hands while he went up the stairs, taking them two at a time to reach the top fast.

I don't wear a watch I don't know how long he was in there, but it couldn't have been more than twenty minutes. Even with a breeze, beads of sweat formed across my forehead; the stifling air swirled around, but not really cooling me off. Smacking my lips, I envisioned a cold drink with lot of ice. Maybe I could dip my feet in the water; after imagining myself falling in, that thought quickly evaporated.

The screen door squeaked opened and snapped shut, Charlie walked back towards me, looking down and watching the steps. Shifting in the boat, I attempted to see his face to read an answer, but I couldn't.

When he reached the boat, he extended his hand to me. "I guess this means we are good to go?" I asked, putting my hand into his.

"Yep. She is extremely excited to talk to you," he told me with a wide smile.

A sigh of relief escaped from my lips. "You had me so nervous!"

"I told you not to worry. Have I told you anything to make you not believe me?"

"No. You have been right on par with everything so far."

"Remember that! Come on," he said, leading me up the stairs, opening the screen door for me to enter first. I stepped into the home of Aunt Nina. Taking a quick second to look around the small room, I noticed the walls were not painted and no pictures were hung, just the beautiful cypress wood grain that served as a work of art. There was one small side table next to an overstuffed recliner. The large uncovered windows next to the main door let in a perfect amount of natural light. A small lamp on the side table was the only lighting for the evenings.

How in the world did she get that chair all the way out here? Surely, no one would deliver it. Everything would have to come by boat. We are out in the middle of nowhere! I thought to myself. I moved my gaze to the doorway leading to the kitchen area.

Aunt Nina stood there watching me. She wore a white lace cloak over her modest clothing. Her tanned skin resembled Charlie's. Her slight smile was glossed with a peach lipstick. Her mascara along with eyeliner was curled up in the edges of her eyes and applied very thickly. Her hands were aged, with heavy veins. As she folded them with her left hand on top, I saw a beautiful turquoise ring on her wedding ring finger.

I thought to myself examining Aunt Nina, *It is way too hot to be wearing a cloak. At least it is lace so it would breathe a little.*

"Tell me what brings you to visit me with such a lovely soul Charlie?" she asked as she motioned for us to follow her.

He spoke as we followed her, "I will let her explain it to you, Aunt Nina." Charlie pulled out a black metal folding chair that had a patchwork cushion on it and sat down. Her ring clinked on the aluminum tabletop as she patted the table and pointed for me to sit as well. I took the dark brown wooden chair across from Aunt Nina. She sat in the wooden chair painted a bright purple color that was closest to the kitchen area.

Clearing my throat, I asked, "I am looking for some guidance. Charlie thought maybe you could help me?" I gave a little smile then bit down on my lower lip and waited for her response.

She adjusted her ring, then folded her hands and placed them carefully on the table in front of her, sitting very tall and head held up high. "Do you know why I live alone out here?" she asked me.

I had no clue other than the cloak. So far, she seemed fairly normal to me, and showed no reason why she wouldn't live with other people. "No."

"I… am a voodoo queen."

My eyebrows arched, showing my look of shock. My head swung quickly to face Charlie. "How could you bring me to the one thing I am trying to flee from? She is a voodoo queen!" I flailed my arm in her direction. "Did you not listen to anything I told you?" I pushed the chair back and began to try to walk out. Charlie rose, grabbing ahold of my arm and putting me back into my chair with a little bit of force. He stood there with his arms folded, blocking my path to leave with a stern look across his face. My jaw dropped and my eyebrows furrowed with disgust.

Twisting around to glare at him, I pulled my arm into my body and leaned as far away from him as I could. Shaking my head at him, I scowled, "How could you?"

Aunt Nina could hear the anger in my voice, she spoke quickly to diffuse me, "Oh child, don't be afraid. I have been practicing voodoo for forty years now," she continued, "and I am a Catholic. There a lot of negative connotations with voodoo since I moved out here and Miranda LaTour started being more public." She fluttered her hand out to dismiss anything that might be troubling me.

My eyes widened as I asked her, "You know Miranda?" Turning back towards Charlie and pointing at Aunt Nina, I said, "She knows Miranda!"

"I told you not to worry," he said with a sigh, "When are you going to start trusting me?"

I looked away, trying to hide my embarrassment. I focused on my hands that were now folded on the table. He had been nothing but helpful. I wish I could just let go and trust him.

"My dear, I know her all too well," Aunt Nina said as she reached across the table and placed her hand over mine.

Looking up, I could see a softness in her eyes and I felt a calm wave over me as I spoke, "Please tell me about her. Tell me everything."

"I will, I promise. But I want to know about you first. Let me know how I can help you," she said as she lifted her hand off mine and rested it back on the table.

I looked at Charlie for courage. Unfolding his arms, he smiled back at me, patting my arm and sitting back into his chair. "Arielle, she can help you. I promise you are safe here. I am right here with you too."

I explained about the visitors, the readings, strange animals, dreams, the hauntings, Papa's book, and everything else I could think of... I told her everything. My mouth was dry from the start. Charlie, being so observant, rose and poured me a glass of sweet tea, placing it down gently in front of me. "Thank you," I said after taking more than half of the glass in two gulps.

Aunt Nina began to explain a few things to me and what I could do to combat Miranda and the dark magic. "You see, Miranda is a normal person just like you and me. Some of it is magic and some of it is real. You need to figure out what is magic and not be afraid of that part of the illusion. There are definitely some real things that gives her powers. You can tap into the other worlds, but you need to be careful of whom you ask to help you because you can really get some evil souls that seem like they are helping you, but really, they are using you to carry out their evil ways that were not finished while they were here alive on earth. You want to surround
90

yourself with your 10,000 angels and ask for God's white light to protect you before you venture into the world of the dead." I nodded while she used her hands in a flowing manner while she talked. "There are angels around us all the time whispering in our ears and guiding us. If you open your mind and your heart, they can tell you many things. Just like people, there are good and bad angels, because they also have a free will to make choices. Angels have a lot of power over the people they are attached to. You still have your own free will, but they can and will try to alter some of your paths. You need to make sure to distance yourself from the fallen angels. Use the white spirits who can guide you away from the black magic."

I responded, "I understand what you are saying to me, but I don't know how to always make that happen. This is so much information."

Aunt Nina told me, "It will be a battle that you will have to fight your whole life. Everyone has the same battle, only because of your gift you will be more in tune to it and able to modify the outcome of the choices being pushed on you."

"How will I do this? How do I know what is real or magic?" I asked in a shaky voice.

Aunt Nina calmly replied, "I am going to teach you everything I know. You also need to learn the name of your angel. Everyone has one angel assigned to them. You want to build a personal relationship with them. Are you ready to learn?"

"Absolutely I want to know everything, right now! I have been feeling so lost I didn't know who to talk to or who to turn to for advice or help. When do we start?"

"There is one very important thing you must remember. Do not let Miranda physically hold onto you for an extended period of time without your enchantment item on you. You want to keep your item touching your body all the time; don't ever take it off. It will not protect you from all evil, but it wards of the vast majority of evil spirits and spells that are cast towards you." She held her cloak out towards me.

"The cloak that you are wearing, it is like Miranda's long dress she wears. This is your enchanted item?" I asked as I lightly touched the edge of her cloak.

Aunt Nina smiled at me. "You are a picking up on things quickly; that is good thing," Aunt Nina told me. "I have 40 plus years of information to pour into you head. We will have to get you your own item soon."

As more and more questions arose, I looked at Charlie. I wondered if he was bored out of his mind listening to the two of us yapping on and on about voodoo and such things. He was leaned back in his chair dozing. Aunt Nina noticed me looking at him.

She cleared her throat loudly and my head snapped back to her, and Charlie started to awake, "Charlie, what do you think about Arielle staying here with me for a few days?"

I opened my mouth to say something to the effect that Charlie is not my keeper and I do what I want to do. But he beat me too it. "She is a grown woman and obviously makes up her own mind," he said as he rubbed the sleep out of his eyes.

I smiled because I liked what he said... I was an independent young lady and nothing was going to stop me from what I want to do, so he was very right. "I left my bag at Charlie's."

"He can bring it back to you tomorrow I have everything you might need here for the night," Aunt Nina suggested.

Smiling at her, I said, "I would like that very much."

Charlie got up and patted me on my shoulder and said to his aunt, "Thank you for taking care of her. I figured you would be the only one who would understand and be able to help her with her gift."

92

Aunt Nina and I stood up and followed him to the door, watching him walk down the stairs to his pirogue. He untied it and started down the waterways. He raised a hand and waved without looking back at us. Still looking at Charlie, I waved, even though I know he didn't see me. I said to Aunt Nina, "I am ready to learn how to protect myself." I was startled when something furry brushed against my leg, causing me to jump back.

A cream and tan striped tabby appeared on the porch, weaving in and out of Aunt Nina's legs. "Hi, Kitty, Kitty," I cooed, bending down to run my hand down his back.

"Here is your first lesson. This cat is a spirit in animal form," Aunt Nina told me as she squatted down next to us and used both hand to scratch under his chin, "He is my spirit guide." He purred loudly at us.

I stood up and looked down at them in amazement. "I had a white dog visit me with a tag. His name was Breeze," I told her as the cat disappeared just like Breeze did; he jumped off the porch and evaporated. "Why do they come? What do they want? That isn't your angel, is it?"

"No, that isn't your angel, that was a spirit guide. It could be someone that has passed on. It definitely is a spirit that is taking the form of an animal, not an angel. They appear at their own will," Aunt Nina told me. "I find they do show up when we need them most. Then sometimes just to remind me they are around, like just now. Oh dear child, you have much more about yourself that you have no idea about," she exclaimed, clapping her hands together and holding them up her mouth. A smile peeked around her hands. "How old are you?" she asked.

"I am nineteen," I said.

"You have a very special gift and Miranda knows it. She wants it for some reason. She will try to steal your gift and could possibly do it too. We need to get you protected and educated before you return home. There might be a lot more to you than meets the eye!" she said. We went inside her home and back into the kitchen.

I am a night owl and it was helpful that Aunt Nina was also. She showed me some of her magic spells. All of them were illusions of smoke and lights. She conjured up some miniature demon skulls, like those that were following me when I was on the motorcycle in town. It was starting to make sense why they would appear and disappear in areas. "The spells will work in a section of space and would either dissipate or not work at all if you are outside the boundaries of the space the spell is cast upon," Aunt Nina explained.

"I am beginning to think Miranda is just a big fake with lots of smoke and tricks that are fooling everyone," I suggested as I floundered around my hands and bobbed my head.

Aunt Nina assured me, "She is still dangerous and not to be taken lightly. She has evil spirits that are using her like a puppet. She thinks she is in complete control; she is not. Don't let your guard down. Be humble. Ask for God to keep you safe at all time. Even if it is just magic, there might be something evil behind it using magic as a disguise to fool you. There are so many layers to everything. It is easy to be fooled."

"What is the difference between voodoo and witchcraft?" I asked.

"Basically, they are different religions. Voodoo has more of the Catholic traits than witchcraft. This is what separates the two religions very pagan traits," she explained.

"I have so many questions it will take years to get them all answered!" I sighed, dropping my shoulders and my face downwards.

As the 2 a.m. hour approached, Aunt Nina wanted to show me what happens at the bewitching hour. "I don't know if you will be able to see it yet. Your mind is still very clouded by worldly things," she said.

I followed her out on the porch. The night air was thick and still. I could hear the lapping on the water on the pilings down by the pier.

"Come with me," she said holding a lantern that cast a warm glow around us. Trusting her, I followed her into the dark night that I feared so much.

CHAPTER TWELVE

Safety In The Darkness

A white sliver of moon hung low in a starry sky, hardly casting any light in the deep swamp. I followed Aunt Nina around the wraparound porch to the other side of the house, down the stairs to the swampy land. She extended her arm holding a dim lantern in front of us guiding our path. This swampland ground was firmer than most areas, but our shoes still squished as we walked. As we traveled down a path into a clearing, my mind wandered to the animals and gators that might be out at night looking for something to sink their teeth into. Following closely behind Aunt Nina, I slid my arm under hers to lock our elbows to stay close to her and avoid stepping on her cloak billowing behind her. She gave me a gentle smile and patted my hand as we continued through the cypress trees towering over us.

When we got to a clearing, she took my hand, placed it on her forearm, and told me, "Hold onto me no matter what, for the next few hours. You might see nothing at all. Since you don't have an enchanted item yet, I wanted to ensure that you will be protected by my enchantments."

"Okay," I whispered.

Standing in the middle of the clearing, I focused my attention on her, avoiding looking into the darkness. She leaned her head back and gazed up at the stars. Following her lead, listening to the silence, I swallowed hard. We stood there for about a minute or two as we saw clouds swirling above our heads.

The winds spoke to me, whispering a name. *Jaaacob.* I turned my head to the left and then to the right, trying to make sense of what I was hearing and seeing. The stars in the sky appeared to get larger, transforming into a variety of colors. The first one I noticed was an ice blue color, then a light pink one, and a brilliant gold one. The stars floated down towards me, increasing in size. I fixated on the colors almost in a trance. Before I knew it, there were hundreds surrounding us. The orbs landed on the ground next to us. The lights were about two or three times the size of an adult human being.

A moment of fear tugged at my heart as I looked at Aunt Nina for reassurance that we were safe and all was well with our experience. Her face broke out with a huge smile and she chuckled. The colors danced off her rounded cheeks to lighten her smile. I wanted to ask her questions, but didn't want to break the splendor around us as I smiled back at her.

Her smile dropped off her face, and she grabbed a hold of my arm, pulling me into her. She wrapped her arms around me. I looked over her shoulder to see the lights around us starting to flicker, some of them zapped out, like you turned off a light bulb. Something happened changing the atmosphere; the air was no longer heavy and thick; a coolness blew around us. My breath pushed out of my mouth and turned white as I shuddered from the cold. Weather changes like this don't happen in Louisiana... ever!

I wrapped my arms around her waist and held on and my brow furrowed in concern. The winds picked up as the lights continued to swirl like a tornado, as my hair whipped up, slapping me in the cheeks. Trying to subdue a bubbling panic attack, I focused on Aunt Nina. Her face remained serious and calm. I watched her eyes narrowing, moving quickly, watching the light sources. Not taking my focus off her, I could see in my peripheral vision the lights one by one extinguished as the darkness returned.

This can't be magic. This part must be real?

My tension and angst mounted as questions filled my mind. A loud clap of thunder erupted and the remaining lights including the lantern instantly were gone. Waiting for my eyes to focus in the dark, I couldn't see Aunt Nina.

Feeling something drag across my leg like fabric, I let out a quiet, "Eek!"

Aunt Nina put her hand on my head, and pressing me to rest my head on her shoulder, I closed my eyes and followed her lead. I curled my hands into fists, but remained holding onto her tightly. I could hear a deep whisper in the winds running over my ears. I opened one eye and glanced around, not moving my head. My eyes had finally adjusted to the darkness and I could make out the tree line around us. There were dark shapes surrounding us gliding by, similar to how a dog would circle its prey.

My fear started to turn into anger, as if, *How dare they mess with us? We are the good guys*!

Aunt Nina reached into her satchel that was looped around her cloth belt and began to toss a dust substance. The figures stopped their movements, but they didn't leave. The large figures with no defined features dark charcoal gray loomed near us. The sound of cats hissing engulfed us. Something cold and numbing latched onto my arm. The feeling moved rapidly up to my shoulder into my neck, Weakened, I tried to cry out as my breathing shallowed. Aunt Nina realized the change in my body going limp as I slid towards the ground. Taking the bag of dust, she dumped it directly on the creature. It let out an ear-piercing screech and let go of my arm, flying into the black sky.

I sucked in a deep breath as my body shook violently and I fell to my knees. Aunt Nina stooped down and draped her cloak around us both. The sounds of growls, hisses, and screeching seemed more distant than before. The low clouds parted as the stars started to twinkle a little light on us.

We were both still under the cloak as Aunt Nina fumbled for a lighter. She flicked it and a few sparks sputtered out; on the third try a small flame was before us. She lit the lantern and removed the cloak from our heads, adjusting the wick on the lantern. Only the dust remained; no more colorful lights, no more creatures. I hesitantly looked around as the lantern flickered brighter, casting our shadows on the trees. Everything appeared to be back to normal.

Aunt Nina rose, with the lantern in one hand, and she offered me her other hand. "Can you stand?"

"Yes, I think so." I took her hand as I rose. As I continued to hold it tight, we made our way back to the camp, constantly glancing over my shoulder. The shock was mentally exhausting, as well as what that creature drained from me. My eyes darted around, looking at the dark trees, waiting for something to grab a hold of me. I felt like a child who was afraid of the dark and wanted my mama to hold me close. Aunt Nina let go of my clutch, putting her arm around me to steady me and using the lantern to illuminate our way. She released me at the base of the stairs. I steadied myself as I took the stairs one at a time up to her camp.

When we reached the top porch, the tabby greeted us. He purred away, starting a chatter of meowing as he rubbed against my legs, as if to say, *It is good to see you made it back okay.* I leaned down and gave him a scratch behind the ears. He immediately flopped down on the porch belly up. I squatted down to smother him in love. He reached up with his paws and grabbed onto one of my hands to pull it towards his head for some more attention.

"This is much better, some normal activity!" I told Aunt Nina as I stood up. The tabby disappeared with a puff of misty smoke. "So much for normal," I said as my body drooped from exhaustion. I stumbled into the porch railing, trying to steady myself.

"Come on inside." She motioned with her hands for me to follow. I zoned out watching her flowing cloak, trying to make sense of everything that just happened. I sat at the kitchen table holding my head in my palms and staring off into space. She started the tea kettle on the stovetop and pulled out two mugs. Straining her neck to look back at me, she asked, "Do you want to talk about this or do you need some time to process everything?"

My face drew a puzzled look across it and I looked up at Aunt Nina, keeping my head still in my palms. "I have no idea what to think or even say. I guess I need some time to figure it all out in my pea brain," I said. "I think I heard my angel's name out there. Before all the light appeared, I think I heard the name Jacob in the winds."

She gave me a gentle smile, placing the hot cup of water in front of me and one in front of her chair. She went back to retrieve a golden tin of tea leaves for us to choose a flavor. "That is quite possible. Your angel will whisper their name to you when the time is right. Which tea would you like?" Sitting down, she opened the tin that had six divided channels. Scooping out the crushed tea leaves, she poured them into the silver ball with a chain clamping it tight. Looking up for my response, she plopped hers into the steaming mug, bobbing it up and down while holding the chain.

"Do you have chamomile? When I would have bad dreams, and couldn't go back to sleep right away, my mom would give me hot chamomile tea. This seems like a bad dream."

"It intrigues me how a relationship can mold us into the people we are destined to become. It sounds like you are close to your mama," Aunt Nina said, trying to keep the subject away from what just happened. "Tell me about your parents."

"My papa kept my mama grounded. He was our family's rock. Our lives have been shaken since we lost him to lung cancer the beginning of this year." My eyes filled with tears as I fought to keep them from running down my cheeks. I blew across the top of the mug to push the steam away then took a large gulp of my tea. Aunt Nina waited for me to compose myself. After a long pause, I continued, "I miss him so much. Mama has disconnected and is grasping to find her way through her grief. I don't expect her to be able to help me right now. She has to help herself find a way to live without him. Mama is up in Michigan on a family reunion and decided to stay a little longer. She is visiting all the old places she and Papa used to go to when they lived up there. I guess that is part of her grieving process."

My arm still hurt somewhat where I was grabbed by that thing. I set my tea down to turn and examine my arm. "There is a mark here! Look!" I extended my arm, hovering across the table for her to get a closer view.

"It looks like the shape of a skeleton handprint," Aunt Nina said holding my arm as she examined the area. "It is red like sunburn and is hot to the touch."

"That is odd because the sensation when I was being held was extremely cold I couldn't stand it, and now it is hot to the touch."

Aunt Nina rotated my arm to view the area one more time. She breezed out of the room and returned with a small orange tin about the size of a compact powder case. Sitting down, she opened the tin. I could see a red symbol on the lid. She put a glob of something that looked like Vaseline on my "infected" area. The coolness quieted the burn. The smell of clover filled my nose.

"Thank you, it is feeling better already. Maybe we can continue our chat tomorrow. I think I need to sleep," I told her, examining at the salve on my arm.

"You had a very eventful day. Sleep would be good for you and we can talk more in the morning." Aunt Nina showed me to the spare room. I didn't even take time to look around to take in the personality of the room. I took off my shoes and climbed into the bed, pulling the patchwork quilt over my head.

I fell into a deep sleep as a man I did not know came to me in my dreams. He didn't speak to me, but showed me some items. One of the items was a fleur-de-lis pendant necklace. He dangled the common symbol in front of my eyes. The middle came to an upside-down teardrop point. On each side the same tear-drop curled downward and was nestled with two small teardrops that curled up around them. He placed it into the palm of my hand, folding my finger around it. He showed me a very small blue velvet cinch bag with old buttons, marbles, screws, and odds and ends. We sat and smiled at each other for a long time; I felt protected.

I awoke extremely late the next day and well rested. I slept so late that the coffee was cold. Charlie was there already with my bag. I could hear his voice traveling down the hallway, but I couldn't hear the conversation. I tried to make myself look presentable before going to the kitchen. Charlie smiled at me and pointed to my bag as he continued to talk to his aunt about the upcoming hurricane season.

"Thank you," I said to him quietly as I started to sneak out of the room with my cup of coffee and bag.

Charlie stopped me and asked, "Hey! Would you like to go out for a boat ride to clear your head?"

"I would like that if you are not too busy today."

"The field trips and tourists are not flocking in yet, so I have plenty of time."

After I ate and cleaned up, we got into his pirogue for a ride.

"I am hopeful for a quiet and uneventful afternoon. I had plenty of excitement yesterday," I admitted to Charlie as he pushed off from the dock the water swirled around the side of the pirogue.

"She told me. I was here very early, so we had plenty of time to catch up while you rested," he said while he looked over my head to see the direction he wanted to steer us in.

"Thank you. Y'all are so very kind. I am so grateful I have someone to talk to that I can not only trust, but learn from."

"God placed you right where he wanted you to be, Arielle. Don't fight his plan."

I nodded as my mind wandered to memories. Sometimes the quiet can be good to get myself grounded, but sometimes I tend to over think things. My papa came to my mind as we glided past the trees. Papa would take us out on the water when we would stay at the camps. I wished he was still here to bounce ideas off of and get advice and, even more, talk about his book. I remember he would check me out of school and we would have lunch. What I liked the most, it was just the two of us. Some days I forgot he was gone. I would think to myself, *Oh, I could meet him for lunch so we can chat about things.* Then reality set in; what a bummer. I miss him so much that my heart aches. The pain forces the tears to flow, then I can't stop them.

Change your topic, Arielle, you don't want to start crying! You need to focus on the now. Use this time to work with Aunt Nina. I hardened my exterior, pushing the sadness away for a later time. I felt like I don't get much of a chance to be a carefree teenager with all these obscure things happening to me, and that burns an anger inside of me. I remind myself this is a blessing and I should be thankful and don't let the darkness and anger take over the good inside of me.

Breaking the silence, I turned around on the small wooden seat to face Charlie, asking, "Why do you think I have these gifts and what am I really supposed to do with them?"

He gave a shrug while paddling. Pausing, he rested the oar across his knees and looked into my eyes. "Arielle, I knew you were different the first time we met. Different in a good way of course." He winked at me. "That is why I like you... You know you are doing an unusual thing when you help others. Just like everyone in this crazy world, we have to find our path. Your path seems a little more important than most people, in my opinion."

His kind words made me blush, I smiled and shifted my eyes away. "I like the idea of being important, but it is scary, because I feel so lost all the time."

"You are not the first person to feel lost and scared. After both my parents died, I was lost, and I blamed God for a few years. I am just coming around to see he has a plan for me too," Charlie said as he swung the paddle across the boat to keep us going in a straight line.

"I really do like helping people. Mom always had me volunteering and thinking outside of the box as to how I can make a difference to help others. I am ready for Him to use me, to show his love to the world through me."

"Arielle, I think He has big plans for you," Before we knew it, several hours had passed as we found ourselves back at the pier at Aunt Nina's camp. He helped me back on the bulkhead and followed behind me, saying, "Do you want me to come back in a couple of days to bring you home?"

"Yes, I would like to stay longer if you don't mind... Thank you, Charlie... Thank you for everything," I said over my shoulder as he followed me up the stairs to the porch. He patted my shoulder, leaving me on the porch watching the peaceful swamp life go by--no people, just the lazy wildlife.

Aunt Nina joined me on the porch as I touched my arm. "How can I protect myself from these demons? What was the dust that you used to ward them off?"

"I take plain red clay pots to be blessed by a priest, and I crush them up to create the dust. The red mimics Jesus' blood, and the demons have no other choice than to retreat when touched by it," she said.

"Whoa! It's amazing how much you have learned. I will need to get some "Pixie" dust," I joked with her.

"A lot of people think that I am evil and do not believe in the trinity--God, Jesus, and the Holy Spirit, because I practice voodoo. Most people, if they do not understand something, they are afraid and assume you are evil. I walk with God. I know that because he has shown me my guardian angel. He has the most beautiful silver wings that reflect my aura, which is silver. Each color reflects something about yourself. Silver means I have great spiritual wealth. I was blessed with my gift and learned very early on how to use it for good. Do you know your aura color?" Aunt Nina asked.

"I didn't even know I had an aura. Can you tell me what color my aura is? And I would like to see my guardian angel too."

"Your aura is an ice blue color, which means you have a nurturing soul, with a halo of light pink, which means you are blessed with a strong clairvoyance and very artistic. I will teach you how to communicate with your angel, but first we will need to get you an enchanted item to help keep you safe from demons and dark spirits," she said as we went inside. She found me lounging in the front room in her overstuffed chair. She dangled a pendant with a chain in front of me.

As soon as I laid eyes on it, I began to stutter, holding my left hand across my chest in disbelief. "I--I--I saw that in my dreams last night. It was the fleur-de-lis pendant necklace! A man visited me and gave me the necklace, and he also showed me a bag of buttons and other items." My hand covered my gaping mouth.

She smiled. "It might be my late husband John. I don't ever see him but feel his presence often. I don't know about any buttons or how to explain what it means. Just be patient. It will be revealed to you when the time is right. Let's make this necklace work for you!" she said. She took my hand away from my mouth and dropped the necklace into my hand and closed my fingers around it just like in the dream. All I could was shake my head in awe.

I followed her into the kitchen. Charlie was still there and had been buzzing around working on something for dinner for us. "He is a good man," she told me as we passed by.

I blushed as I locked eyes with him. *Why am I blushing? It's just Charlie.*

Drifting behind, I followed Aunt Nina into her bedroom where she dug around in a cabinet. "I have all your items. Are you ready to go outside for the enchantment spell?"

"As ready as I am ever going to be!"

CHAPTER THIRTEEN
The Book Returns

I bounced out the back of the house and down the stairs. We walked to the same area where all the excitement happened last night. "This looks very different in the daytime," I said. She had a garden area with lots of flowering plants. I pointed to the crop of veggies. "I guess you learn to be self-sufficient living this far out from everything?"

"I could live completely off my land if I had to, but don't get me wrong; I go into the nearest town to fetch gas station donuts at least once a week. And I don't grow my own coffee beans. There are some things you don't mess with; you just buy them, coffee and donuts."

Her realness made me smile and draw closer to her.

Aunt Nina walked over to a small hand-built wooden table and placed the items on the table. The items scattered as she took time to organize them. First, she put down a piece of fabric with the image of the Blessed Mother Mary. Next she placed three white candles at different points, creating a triangle. Being a great teacher, she took the time to explain what she was doing and the history behind the ritual.

"The three white candles represent the Trinity. We call upon God, Jesus, and the Holy Spirit to be present and guide us and keep us safe from any evil demons that might interfere with the work we are trying to do in God's white light," Aunt Nina said.

I nodded as she explained further.

"The way spirits work, they can cross in front of each other and you may not know who you are speaking to, and they possibly could be something that is not surrounded with the white light."

Aunt Nina took her time to make sure that we were safe before calling upon any spirits or begin a ritual.

"Aunt Nina," I began, "thank you for helping me. I feel safe with you and trust you completely. Really, I don't have anyone else to turn to, so I am thankful that you are an honest and faithful person to guide me while I am still learning."

She continued setting up on the small table but paused to smile at me. "Arielle, I am happy God brought you to me. I didn't have anyone else to pass on my knowledge to!"

"Should I be taking notes? I never was good at taking notes in school. I learned much better with hands-on type of work."

"There is a time for notes, but I think you are okay for now. You will want to write down your experience. Most of us do and keep it locked to pass on to someone."

"Should I start mine now?"

"Absolutely!"

I could hear the mid-afternoon swamp sounds, frogs and crickets randomly sounding off. A few brown pelicans breezed overhead searching for their last meal of the day over the lake. I clasped my hands together, holding them to my chest and waiting for her instructions.

Once Aunt Nina was satisfied with the location of the items, she asked me, "Please stand on my right side, in front of the table." She took my hands and placed a pack of matches in them as I took my position. She asked me, "Will you light each candle starting with the one in front of me and working clockwise to the other two candles?"

I nodded as I struck the match and leaned in to light the first white candle.

She chanted a loud, "O Lord, I call upon the Holy Spirit to come bless this candle to start the first part of the Trinity here with us. O Lord, be with us, guide us today."

I waited for her finish and then moved on to the next candle. I blew out the match and toss it on the soft ground, then retrieved a fresh match each time, repeating the motions to light the next candle.

Aunt Nina continued, "O Lord, I call upon Jesus to come and bless this candle to complete the second part of the Holy Trinity here with us."

A large flame arched from the match as it touched the third candle, lighting it.

She chanted again, "O Lord, I call upon God to come and bless this candle to complete the final part of the Holy Trinity here with us."

The sun dipped behind a cloud, casting a shadow upon us as a hot breeze ran through the trees. The flames flickered but did not blow out. Aunt Nina took out her bag and dusted a circle area around us with the red clay pieces and returned to the front of the table next to me. She folded her hands in prayer and called again upon God, "Lord God, bless us while we are here today."

She placed the necklace in the left palm of my hand, folding my fingers closed just like in my dream. She then took a strip of white material and wrapped it around the hand like a mummy. She sprinkled holy water on top of my wrapped hand. She tucked a feather in the white wrapping where the flowing part stuck out.

"Is this feather from a white pelican or an egret?" I asked, lightly swishing the feather around.

"Neither. This is from a white-tailed kite. Hold still." She placed my hand back on the table.

Thankfully, the sun was still hidden behind a cloud, giving a little shade so it wasn't quite so stifling outside. A low clap of thunder echoed in the distance. Looking towards the sky, I hoped we wouldn't get rained on.

Aunt Nina moved my hand to the center of the table while the three candles flickered around it. "We will be done before the rain comes," she assured me. I focused on what she was doing. She opened another bag with fine tan powder in it. Tossing the mixture over the candles, they flared up wildly.

"Whoa!" I exclaimed, leaning away, afraid that the white cloth might catch on fire with my hand in there. I steadied my breathing, keeping my hand where it was and trying to remain calm. The flames shot up about three feet into the sky. Interestingly I didn't feel any heat from the flames. Instead there was a cool breeze that made my hair fly up and dance around my rosy cheeks. Over the candles I spotted a playful small orb bouncing around in the air. It glowed a beautiful color and flickered in the daylight, pulsing from a light pink to a darker pink. A few other orbs appeared, golden and light blue and drifting in the sky. The flames grew in length until they were three thin strings of bright white flames extended to the heavens above. My eyes followed the flames as I gazed up, lost in the moment and full of peace.

Out of the corner of my eye, a dark silhouette figure with a fur lining around its neck appeared to the left side of me. I jumped, almost pulling my hand away from the table. When I quickly turned to see the figure, it dissipated. I snapped my head back, looking at Aunt Nina to see if she saw the figure too. She didn't because she had her eyes closed and was deep in prayer. The pink orb began to fade, and the flames started to come back down from the sky. The sun peeked out from a cloud as the sounds of thunder rolled closer.

Walking around to the last candle I lit, Aunt Nina said, "Thank you, God, for being present." Then blowing out the candle with her hand cupped around it, she walked to the middle candle. "Thank you, Jesus, for being present," she said, extinguishing the candle the same way. As she approached the last candle, the dark figure appeared to her. The fur on its neck extruded like a scared cat. She drew a breath and threw the whole bag of red clay at it. The figure didn't move nor make a sound.

I remained still, examining the figure, trying to see a face. It was a dark, transparent figure. I could see a dark glowing red area where eyes should be. I began to tremble as I prayed *God, Jacob, and all the angels, come keep us safe!* My hand lay on the table, not knowing what to do since the last candle was still light.

Aunt Nina quickly blew out the candle and loudly proclaimed, "Thank you, Holy Spirit, for being present today." As the words left her mouth, a white blinding, solid flash about a foot in diameter came down from the sky and hit the ground where the figure stood. The light scorched the ground, leaving black singe marks, and tiny flames danced on the grassy area. The figure was toast and the light evaporated. The smell of burnt grass and leaves filled my nose as Aunt Nina took my wrist, tugging me back swiftly to the camp. We left all the items on the table. The sky rumbled; fat, cold raindrops poured out of the sky, smacking down hard on us before we could make it all the way to the porch.

We were not completely drenched, but enough to have a little chill from going from the heat of the afternoon to the cold splash of the rain. Standing with our backs against the house, in silence, we watched the rain come down with full force. It lasted about ten minutes, then it cleared up as the sun started to peek around the dark clouds.

She turned to me and said, "I think it is time you start talking to your angel. He can help warn you of creatures."

All I could do was nod in agreement. I still had my hand wrapped; the poor feather was limp from being caught in the rain. Aunt Nina laughed at how funny it looked. Taking my wrist, she pulled out the feather and gently unwrapped my hand. Unfolding my hand, she took the necklace and clipped it around my neck, resting her hands on my shoulders. My eyes met hers as she smiled, pleased with our accomplishment.

110

The aroma of dinner greeted us as the front door as we moved into the kitchen, Charlie had everything set. After the blessing I began quizzing Aunt Nina. "What was that figure and why didn't the red clay work the same as it did on the other demons? I have never seen figure. The fur around its neck was weird, too, wasn't it?"

"This was a first for me as well. I don't want to say anything until I know what it is for sure."

"Why do you look worried? Should I be worried?" I looked from her to Charlie. He had his head down, steadily eating his shrimp étouffée creation.

"When do you plan on going back to the city?" she asked, not answering my questions.

"I really don't know. I am not in any rush other than to contact Mama and let her know I am all right. I would like to stay a little longer, if that's okay with you? And it looks like my next task is to learn how to communicate with my angel, Jacob... right?"

"You can stay as long as you want to. Yes, we need to work on this right away."

Charlie rose and picked up his plate and Aunt Nina's, asking, "So, when should I come back to pick you up and bring you home?"

"Three more days. Then I will face what was going to happen to me at home."

Charlie nodded as he started towards the sink with the dinner dishes after collecting my empty plate too. "Do you need anything before I head back home for the night?"

"No. I can't think of anything. Dinner was amazing again." I smiled at him.

"Sorry, I meant Aunt Nina. Do you need anything? I can wash the dishes," Charlie said.

"Oh," I said quietly. *Jeez, Arielle, the world doesn't always revolve around you!*

"You head on home. We have everything under control here." He gave his aunt a kiss on the cheek goodbye and waved to me, leaving before the sun dipped down too low.

I hopped up and rushed to the kitchen to clean up before Aunt Nina had time to even object.

I took the time with Aunt Nina very seriously. I wanted to get as much info as possible. That night we made red clay dust for me to keep with me. "Aunt Nina, tell me about the orbs we saw the other night."

"Those orbs are real spirits. Everyone has a colored aura. The first color you noticed reflects your own spirit. The colors to follow can be people you know that have passed on that are there to either communicate with you or watch over you. They can also be angels. Each person has about 10,000 angels assigned to watch over them. Angels are very different in appearance than you would think. They do have wings, and the span of their wings depends on the works they have done to honor God. If an angel appears to you in its normal form, you would probably drop from fear. It is not that they are ugly; they would just be too much for our human brains to understand. When God lets angels appear to humans, he has them take other forms such as animals or even the traditional white robed humans with wings. If an angel has a message for us from God and we pass out, then they are not able to complete their task and "earn" their wings, so God granted them the ability to metamorphose their bodies." Aunt Nina continued, "I have never seen an angel in the original form so I couldn't tell you what one would look like. I have encountered animals that are angels or spirits."

"I am trying to make sense of everything, it's all so bizarre."

"I know, but you need to know all of this stuff. Let me explain a few more things." She continued, "A spirit is a soul of someone who was once here on earth and has passed on. An angel was never human and is God's servant if they so choose or else, they become a fallen angel and serve the devil." She continued, "The dark forms which surrounded us last night--these were either evil spirits or fallen angels. I can't tell you which one I saw because angels can take the form of a spirit. Chances are they were evil spirits sent out by Miranda to try to locate you. Miranda is probably under the control of demon angels. The demon angels hate God and don't want any good things to happen to his beloved people."

"It sounds like they battle every day to pull people over to the dark side and brainwash them into doing their will."

Aunt Nina agreed, saying, "Miranda may or may not even know she is on the dark side. There is something special about you, Arielle. The devil knows it, and I can tell he wants to either convert you away from God or maybe take your gifts. The creature that took a hold of your arm, that was not a spirit, and the fur one today, they were demon angels working for the devil."

I asked her, "How can you tell the difference? It all seems so cloudy to me."

"Angels possess a lot more power than spirits. Spirits can make you feel things, like how they died or how they feel. Or they can give you messages for people who are still here on earth. They cannot directly harm you. Angels are on a different level. They can, if you let them, seize you and take over your body and soul and make you do things to harm others. This is very dangerous and is difficult to get the possessed back without help from either clergy or someone who practices with God's white light spirits," Aunt Nina explained. "I have been able to help several people who have had family members taken over by a fallen angel. Each one had their own struggles, but I was able to bring them back to their former self. Arielle, I want you to learn how to do this then you can help people,

113

maybe even help Miranda, God willing!" My mind raced thinking of all the possibilities. "Come with me to my library. I have some old books I would like to share with you." She brought out her most cherished book. "This is the one I wrote about myself. You need to start your own legacy book."

She handed the book to me, and I traced the cover and said, "This looks like the book my papa left for me."

Her face lit up. "Do you have the book with you?"

My shoulders dropped. "No. I had it but couldn't figure out how to open it, and I think Miranda stole it from me."

"How can you be sure she has it?" Aunt Nina asked.

"Well, when I was escaping out of town, she flashed before me and I saw her with the book. I don't know how to get it back from her."

"Are you sure she didn't return it?"

"How would I even know she returned it?" I replied with a slight tone of annoyance for such a silly question.

"I bet she couldn't open it either and is waiting for you to get it open," Aunt Nina guessed. "It is a really old spell. When she flashed the book at you, she was repositioning its placement. Check your bag that Charlie brought to you."

I rose and we walked to the guest room. I opened the bag, shaking it upside down and dumping everything onto the bed. The book plopped out onto the bed; it was glowing again. I looked at Aunt Nina with my mouth wide open in awe.

She clapped her hands around her mouth, showing the sides of her smile. "Oh this is grand! Open it, child, open it! The book glows when it needs to tell you something."

"I don't know how to open it," I told her.

"Your papa didn't leave anything to help you figure out how to open it?"

"Like what?"

"It could be anything. Just because it is a lock doesn't mean you need a real key. It could be a phrase, an item, really anything. Think, child, is there anything that came with the book?" she asked me.

"There was a bottle of hyssop oil in the box with the book along with my boogieman spray." The book started to move and shake on the bed. I looked at Aunt Nina. "What do I do now?"

"Say *boogieman* again."

"Boogieman." Nothing happened.

"Try saying *hyssop*," she instructed.

"Hyssop." The book shook again, keeping my eyes fixated.

She darted out of the room and came back with a small amber bottle and handed it to me.

"What exactly is hyssop oil and what do I do with this?"

"It is my hyssop oil. It is a biblical oil for purification. It is your key!" she exclaimed.

I pushed all the other items away from the book and stood over the bed, looking down at the book. "Should we maybe go to the table or something?" I asked.

"Good idea." She took the oil back, and I picked up the vibrating book as it tugged at me pulling me down the hallway towards Aunt Nina.

Both of us stood over her small kitchen table as I placed the book in the middle. She carefully handed the oil to me. The book still pulsed a blue glow. I carefully twisted off the cap and placed it on the table. Looking up at Aunt Nina, she looked like a kid at Christmas waiting for the presents to be opened. I bit down on my lower lip and straightened my arm over the book and tilted the bottle. A single drop of the oil formed on the edge of the bottle like thick syrup. The drop released from the bottle and traveled down to the cover of the book. Upon contact, the clear drop transformed into a brilliant, shimmering gold. The thick outside logo circle glowed red; the color traveled to the horizontal line through the middle. The book levitated off the table and turned over the small padlock that required a key, popped open, and dropped to the table. The book gently landed and casually opened to the first page. I couldn't take my eyes off the book.

"I will leave you alone," Aunt Nina said as she slipped out of the kitchen giving my shoulder a light squeeze.

"Thank you." I whispered and slowly sat down holding the open book close to my heart. It was so worn the edges and corners were a lighter color. The cover had a bit of a curve to it from being held open while he wrote in it.

Closing my eyes, I held the book up to my nose, I could see him in my mind and smell his cologne. We walked together down our street away from our home. He held my hand; it was just the two of us. I could see us strolling towards Café Du Monde for coffee and beignets. I could even taste the warm soft dough-like pastries with powdered sugar. I could feel the warmth of the sun on my face as we walked there.

I miss having him here, especially now that I know he was more like me than I ever knew. I gently placed the book on the table; the page flipped towards the middle end of the book and rested.

My dearest Arielle, if you are reading this, I am not here with you in the earthly world anymore. I will miss you, my sweet girl. You know now you are blessed with something very special. Use this book to learn more about me and it will help you on your own journey as well. There is no right or wrong place to start this book. It contains random things that have occurred in my life as well as the lives of my friends and foes. Just remember I will always be close watching over you and doing my best to protect you. Listen for my voice; like a comforting breeze, I am here with you.

As I closed my eyes, Papa was there. We were at the cafe and he told me, "Arielle, you have incredible strength and you are the one to keep the family strong and together."

"Papa, I can't do this without you. I need you here more than God does!"

Papa breathed deeply. "Elle, you have some special gifts, and I will always be here to guide you, even when you feel all alone." He held my hand for a moment and then picked up a beignet and blew the powdered sugar at me. Our laughter echoed in my ears as I began two wake up, my face planted in the book where I had fallen asleep. Some of the ink smeared from the stray tears that escaped.

Holding the book close, I whispered, "I miss you, Papa." Climbing into bed, I cradled the book like a cherished stuffed animal.

CHAPTER FOURTEEN

Trust Me

My shoulder gently shook. "Let's take a trip. There is someone I would like you to meet. Bring your book with you. I would love for you to share what your papa wrote about, if you feel comfortable."

I still had the book under my arm as I rolled over in the bed. "I don't mind talking to you about it, but I don't know about anyone else. I just don't know who to trust."

"He is someone who can help you even more than I can, trust me."

"I do trust... *you.*"

We left at daybreak... I was glad to have a cup of coffee before we left because I'd been so engrossed in Papa's book I stayed up way too late. The tabby sat watching us board Aunt Nina's small boat. I was happy to see she had a small outboard motor attached. This would make the trip faster than just paddling. I took the front bench. As I sat, I wrapped my hand around my necklace to make sure it was still there and held the book tight to my chest. Bending down, she pulled hard as the motor began to purr with a slight cough.

Aunt Nina positioned herself on the back seat and reached behind her to grab hold of the arm sticking out of the motor to steer us to our destination. The slight coolness in the breezy air was refreshing and helped me dust away the sleepiness still in my eyes.

As we traveled in the curves and bends on the waterway, I wondered, *How in the world does anyone really know where they are going? There are so many dead ends. The way the water cuts, it changes the passageways so they are not always the same from year to year either. Maybe one day I will get it.* I am not bad with my sense of direction when I am paying attention and not daydreaming.

Gazing around, I saw the sunrise in all its splendor. It was lovely to see, but not something I plan on doing often. The sky had a pink glow, casting a cherry look to the swamp. The sun rises and sets fast here so it's nice to savor its wonder when you can. Some birds rustled around, looking for their morning food. In the shallow parts of the swamp you can see the egrets gingerly wading in the water, searching for a small fish to nab. There is something majestic to me about birds. I never had any birds growing up, but I like to watch them hunt, fly, even flutter around in the water. The hum of the motor gets the attention of the birds. Most of them take flight before we are too close.

"I want you to work on something for me," Aunt Nina said over the sound of the little outboard motor.

"All right, I am willing to work hard, I promise."

"Find some quiet time and call for your guardian angel to speak to you and verify his or her name. You will get your confirmation that the name is correct because within three days the name will appear to you four times. Just make sure you ask for your guardian angel. We don't want any other evil spirits trying to intercept your message and deceive you! You said you heard the name Jacob, but you want to be certain."

"I can do that. That seems so simple. There isn't anything extra I should be doing?"

"No, it is pretty straight forward, but just listen with your heart and not your mind. Names might come to you, but they won't be right until you get your confirmations."

Aunt Nina slowed the engine, taking a wide turn to the right, to the left a pier came into view. The wake behind us disappeared as we slowed down. As we approached, I leaned to grab a hold of the old pier, hopeful I didn't get any splinters. Once steady, Aunt Nina stepped out to tie down the boat with the small rope connected to the tarnished cleat on the side of the boat. My stomach notified me it was thinking about our next meal. *I wonder if we will be eating here.* We stood on the pier looking up at the house. A man exited and raised a hand to give us a little wave.

He was dressed in all black with a white square collar. This was way out of my home parish; I was not familiar with this priest. "A priest? I don't want to be rude, but I am not sharing my experiences with a priest! Why did you bring me here? I trusted you!" I held tight to my papa's book, wondering, *How could I be so stupid?*

"Don't let the collar fool you, child. I wouldn't throw you to the wolves." She left me standing there and went to greet him.

I took a moment to collect myself and climbed the stairs, breaking a little a sweat. The coolness of the early morning was gone. The weather toyed with me about being cooler, but it was too soon in the season.

"Father Verum, this is Arielle," said Aunt Nina.

After we shook hands, he extended his arm, and with a gliding motion, pointed towards the door, saying, "Welcome."

"Thank you," I said, not making eye contact because I was nervous. Aunt Nina paused for me go inside first. I didn't know what direction to go, so I scooted over to let them both pass. We walked to the kitchen and sat down. A familiar place Southerners usually congregated, the kitchen.

Father Verum and Aunt Nina spent several minutes catching up on things. It sounded like it had been several months since they had seen each other. I took the time to look around. He had a modest living as most did in this area. He did have a collection of mason jars on a shelf. I couldn't quite tell what was in the jars. I looked over the doorways and noticed there were small crucifixes positioned in the middle over the doors.

When the conversation paused, I asked, "May I use the bathroom?"

He directed me with the point of his hand. "Down the hall, first door on the left."

"Thank you." I was so awkward I bowed at the table when I left and scooted off. I made sure to bring my papa's book with me. It was still securely tucked under my arm since I first got off the boat.

I placed the book on the counter next to the sink. After I finished my business, I looked deeply in the mirror at my image. My eyes looked a little more rested than they had in the past few months. I thought I really could use a new lipstick color when I got back to town. I made some puckered lips in the mirror, looking at the color and turning my head from side to side, looking at my reflection.

As I goofed off in the mirror, a flash of small lights caught my eye in the mirror. The lights were grouped behind me off to the left of my shoulder. They shone a bright indigo color. I turned around quickly to double check what I was seeing; nothing was there behind me. With my back to the mirror, I considered just walking out and not looking at the mirror again.

I couldn't help myself; I turned and faced the mirror. The lights were there but grew dim in density. I blinked, fluttering my eyes and leaning in towards the mirror to see if they were indeed there. They remained; some faded and became brighter; some remained constant. They were the size of small Christmas lights. My concentration was broken by a knock at the door. I looked at the door and rapidly looked back at the mirror. The lights stretched out like long pieces of spaghetti and disappeared into the mirror.

"Everything okay in there?" Aunt Nina asked.

"I'm coming. I'm fine, thank you." I ran the water over my hand again so it sounded like I was not just playing in the bathroom like a child.

Aunt Nina was back in the kitchen with Father Verum when I hurried down the hallway. They both were sitting there quietly.

I wondered, *How long was I gone?*

As Father Verum started, I could see a slight smile under his white short beard that matched his white hair. "I wanted to talk to you a little. Aunt Nina was explaining about your unique situation."

"I was surprised she even told you. Most of the people of the cloth I have encountered do not want to discuss any of these types of things," I said matter-of-factly. "We are opening up a pipeline to the devil. With the help of Aunt Nina, I am now understanding why most religious people stay away. It is because they do not know how to use the gifts in God's white light."

He didn't respond to me but instead asked, "Would you like to receive communion while you are here?" He was trying to ease my tension.

A little taken aback by the offer, I paused to think, and said, "Yes, Father, I would."

"Is there anything you would like to confess before communion?" he asked.

"Is this some kind of trick?" I skeptically asked.

"No, Arielle, if you are really Catholic then you do recall that you must confess your sins before you break the bread."

"God knows my heart and my sins that I have to confess."

He chuckled. "You sound like a Lutheran! Very well." He came back to the table and broke bread. Praying over it, he gave it to me and Aunt Nina along with the consecrated wine.

122

Not having eaten anything since last night, I could feel the wine give a slight burn going down my throat. I folded my hands after taking the sacraments, asking God in my silent prayer, *Keep watch over me and guide me in everything that I do. Thank you for giving me your grace, which I do not deserve.* When I raised my eyes, everyone was still in prayer. I could feel the book pulsing again under my arm. Turning the symbol towards my body to hide the cover, I waited until they were finished, and said, "Thank you."

"The gift of communion is always available to you, my child," he responded.

A soft breeze flew through the kitchen as I drew a deep breath. My hair danced around my face; the sides of the book began to shine bright blue. There was no hiding it anymore.

"The Holy Spirit is with you," he said with a soft smile, raising his fluffy white eyebrows.

The refreshing breeze continued to swirl my hair. I could see the same orbs that were in the mirror dancing before my eyes. Focusing on the lights, my company disappeared from my view. As the lights faded, the breeze escaped from the room. I realized Aunt Nina and Father Verum saw the lights too. He clapped his hands together, bringing them up to his lips to cover his gaping mouth. They both looked at each other, smiling like kids on Christmas morning seeing the tree all lit up with pretty packages wrapped up with sparkling bows nestled underneath.

"There is something special about you, kid," Father Verum said, reaching both arms towards me as if he was about to hug me.

"That is great, but what exactly am I doing with all this specialness?" I asked with a smirk.

"It is your quest to figure that out, but sounds like you have a nemesis already with Miranda. Your papa's book might have some good advice since you will have similar gifts."

I gave him a half smile, nodding my head sideways, "Did you know my papa?"

"Yes, I knew your papa. He was a remarkable man. Let me know if he talks about me in his book. I would love to know if he did." He handed me a card with his phone number on it. "Have you learned anything new from his writings?"

"I will let you know, for sure, if he mentions you." The book looked normal again as I opened it, slightly sliding his card inside. "Um, I am not sure yet. There is a lot I don't understand."

"All I can do is pray for you, give you communion, and bless items for you. I do not do spells or anything of that nature. That is not in my doctrine to do such things. You will find none of the priests will consult with you, except Father Beau at Saint Genevieve Church. Don't bother asking any of the others. They will shun you and make sure everyone else does too," he said, shaking his finger at me to emphasize his point.

"I remember when I spoke of some of these things as a child and was told to hush it up and don't bring it up again," I told him, holding my head down in shame.

He nodded. "Father Beau and I are a rarity and have to keep it secret. There are a lot of documented reasons to keep people like you in God's white light. God touched you for a reason. I pray you find your path and remain safe."

He handed Aunt Nina several red terra cotta pots stacked together, then as he handed me the same amount, we shuffled towards the door. *No lunch?* We walked down to the pier to put the pots in the floor of the boat. Turning back to wave goodbye, he made the sign of the cross at us as we launched the boat.

"How about some lunch?" she asked me.

"I thought you would never ask!" I replied, patting my tummy.

Heading in a different direction, we arrived a few minutes later, and she tied the boat on an old dock. We entered from the back entrance into a small restaurant called Vera's and found a two-seater table. I placed the book on the table, cover side down. The waitress came to the table and dropped off some hot French bread with two waters. I forgot to pray I was so hungry. I took my first bite without any butter spread on it just to get something in my stomach.

Aunt Nina bowed her head and said the table prayer out loud; with my mouth full of bread I mumbled along with her. It must be Monday because the same lady came back and dropped off two plates of red beans and rice, which is traditionally served on Monday in South Louisiana. I cleaned my plate by using the French bread to wipe off any little bit of the sauce that was left. Aunt Nina left two small bottles on the table as payment and we headed out.

By the time we got home, it started to get a little dusky and the clouds bubbled up as it threatened to rain again. "That was an interesting day. I am sorry I doubted you."

"I know you are still learning who to trust. I understand. I don't know how many more things I am going to be able to teach you. But I remember I was alone when I learned about my gift too. It sounds like your papa's book will be another good guide. I am sorry he didn't get to tell you in person," she said.

I felt the burn behind my eyes trying to hold the tears back, "At least Father Beau is nearby if I need anything, too."

"I think you should visit Father Beau as soon as you get back to town. You make him aware that you will be needing to get red clay pots to smash up into powder," she told me.

"How is that conversation going to start?" I asked.

"Father Verum will contact him and let him know you are emerging as a new voodoo queen."

"I think I would prefer voodoo princess," I laughed.

I practiced some of the protective spells with Aunt Nina watching me at the kitchen table. "I still don't know my goals other than keeping myself away from harm and keeping my gift from possibly being stolen."

"Those are some pretty large tasks for a new voodoo princess. Your gift can be stolen. Don't forget that! Keep your enchantment close at all times," she warned me.

"How exactly can someone steal my gift? I don't understand how that is done."

"Do you remember the feeling you got when we were in the field?" She tapped on my arm where the burn marks began to fade.

"How could I forget?"

"Your gifts are like surges of energy. They move like current and can be released out of your body. Something was tapping into you to steal the energy from you," Aunt Nina explained.

"That makes sense. So, does the enchantment help hold my energy in or just keep the bad stuff away?" I asked.

"In theory, your enchantment will protect you, so whatever you need, the necklace will provide. Imagine that God has a force field wrapped around you. Your enchantment works though Him."

The day went by all too quickly, and the soft warm blanket of night began to cover the camp. Aunt Nina asked, "Do you want to go out to the field again and see if anything happens?"

We had not gone back out there since the enchantment ritual and the meeting of the dark figure with the fur neckline. "Yes, I want
126

to face things with someone else by my side in case I needed any assistance."

She found her lantern to bring with us. I could smell the sulfur from the match spark as the tip of the match struck the box. Twisting the dial to make the wick on the lantern extend and give us a large circle of light, Aunt Nina asked me, "Do you have your necklace?"

"Check!" I gave her a thumbs up.

"Do you have your red clay?" she asked, looking at me sideways.

"Check!" I gave her a double thumbs up.

"Okay, then let's go." Her white cloak billowed behind her as she descended the stairs. Scanning the sky as we moved to the clearing, I could see the moon was more than a sliver tonight. The small, scattered, puffy clouds reflected off the dim moonlight.

We positioned ourselves in the middle of the area and waited. Nothing happened; in silence we continued to wait. After about an hour's time, I saw a sea blue light in the distant sky. My face drew a huge smile. The other orbs followed, floating around and casting soft colors on us. Aunt Nina's face was glowing in a rainbow of colors from the reflections. I felt so peaceful and connected with everything in the world and beyond. The colors gently faded away as we stood there waiting for something bad to happen next. Nothing. After about another hour, Aunt Nina broke the silence. "Let's head back in the house." She took my hand and patted it gently as we walked back to her home.

"Why did the demons come the first time but not this time?" I asked as we climbed the stairs that creaked underneath our damp shoes.

"They know you are becoming stronger in your faith, and your gift is protected so they are not confronting you," she said.

I was feeling confident, with the tune of the song "Eye of the Tiger" playing in my head. I felt like doing a little shadow boxing like I had mad skills now and could take on anyone or anything! A little confidence is good with a sprinkle of humility to keep you in check. "That is good to know! Maybe they will stay away and I don't have to do anything after all?" I asked hopefully.

Aunt Nina shattered the song in my head. "Nice try, but that won't happen. Evil doesn't just give up. You need to keep your guard up at all times."

CHAPTER FIFTEEN

Breeze, In My Life

Settling in the kitchen, Aunt Nina caught me completely off guard. "Do you have a boyfriend back in the city?"

I blushed, hiding my slight smile with my hand. "I don't have anyone interested in me right now."

Aunt Nina gave me a wink and said, "I think otherwise."

I couldn't wipe the smile off my face thinking of the possibilities. "Wait, are you talking about Charlie?" My face changed to a shocked look with a bit of confusion.

"He is a good man," she reminded me, resting her chin on her fingertips and leaning in towards me for an answer.

"Yes, he is a good man," I agreed with her. "But Charlie is my brother's friend," I explained, shaking my head and waving my hand to dismiss the thought from my head.

She just smiled. "You should try to get a good night's sleep. He will be here in the morning to bring you home. I will make a big farewell breakfast for you before you go with lots of coffee."

"I have a ton of questions for you, not that I know what they are right now, but how will I get in contact with you since you don't have a phone?"

"Charlie," she said, "He will get word to me. If I am ever in the city, I will stop by and visit you as well."

"Okay." I nodded with a little disappointment.

"Get some rest, child."

I was hopeful for a peaceful night's sleep since I was returning home to my normal disruptions. Sleep came and so did the visitors... I walked in a field of lavender; the smell filled my nose as I ran my fingers over the tops of the stalks. The glare from the sun caused me to hold my hand up to block out the rays.

My hand created a silhouette so dark it looked like an oil spill pouring off my hand and filling the entire sky. Not able to see anything, I knew I was still in the field because of the lavender scent. I tried to walk but couldn't feel my feet. The numbness crept up my legs, causing me to fall to my knees.

I was still in complete darkness when a small blue light floated down and landed on my forehead. The light lifted me up, and my feet hovered above the ground. As I continued to rise, I focused on the light and not the lingering fear of not being on the ground. A wind blew past my body, whipping my hair up as something flew by. The blue light flickered; I dropped a little bit. The feeling in my stomach fell to my feet, causing me to lose focus on the orb. Suspended in space the creature flew by, rattling me as I dropped again. The light grew dim and I cried out, "Don't you drop me!" The light glowed brighter. With one hard blow the creature knocked the light out. Arms flailing, I screamed until I slammed into the ground.

Jolting awake, I sat up in bed and tried to locate the smell. I pulled a strand of purple lavender from my hair. I frantically patted around the bed to make sure Papa's book was still there. Placing it gently on the nightstand next to the digital clock that glowed red numbers 6:03 a.m., I gathered my thoughts. *I am up, I might as well go shower and get ready for the day.* Refreshed from my shower, I entered the kitchen and was pleasantly surprised to see Charlie. He stretched out his hand and offered me a white mug full of coffee. He could see my eyes smiling at him over the brim of the cup as I took my first sip.

After the sip, I said, "Thank you and good morning."

"Nice to see you up this early," he said as he casually leaned against the counter sipping his coffee.
130

The three of us sat at the kitchen table. I could tell Aunt Nina wanted to say something because the two of them kept looking at each other with an odd look on their faces.

"What are you two scheming?" I asked them with a mouth full of waffles as the sticky syrup dripped down my chin.

Aunt Nina spoke first. "I was thinking maybe Charlie should go stay with you at your mama's house for a while. Just until, you know, things are going to be okay with you. Not that he can repel spirits or anything like that, but maybe having someone in the house would deter people from bothering you."

I gave Charlie a crooked smile to see if I could read his face. The small smile on his face convinced me that, yes, he didn't mind. I asked him, "What about your business? Shouldn't you be getting things ready for the upcoming season?"

The smile faded and a half frown formed as he let out a big, "Naaah! Anyway, my cousin Nick can handle all the prep work, no big deal," he said with a dismissing hand wave.

"Well, if you feel that it's best, I will agree to it."

Both Aunt Nina and Charlie nodded a yes towards me. "Do you have your things packed up?" Charlie asked as he began to pick up the dishes.

"Not quite, I have a few things to toss in my bag then I will be ready." I rose to put my coffee cup in the sink, bumping into Charlie a little because the kitchen was so small. I kept my head down to hide any feeling I might be having and went to the guest room to gather my things.

Charlie was down at the pier when I came out. Taking a moment with Aunt Nina and giving her a long hug, I said, "Thank you for everything... I don't want to leave you."

She placed her hands around my shoulders and looked me square in the eye. I could see my reflection in her dark brown eyes. "You need to go home. Your mama is probably worried sick. She hasn't heard from you in days. Promise me you will contact Charlie if you need anything from me and come to visit often to tell me everything you are learning about your gifts."

I nodded and said, "I promise."

She released me, then hugged me again, "Send Arielle's 10,000 angels to protect her from evil and demons. Guide her on this journey to find her purpose from You. Amen!"

"Amen!" Pinching my pendant, I kissed it, showing her I was wearing it.

"Read your papa's book!" she called to me and waved as we pushed off. I waved back a little too frantically, wobbling the boat. Grabbing the sides, I sheepishly smiled at Charlie. *Why am I such a klutz?* The ride back started very quiet.

About thirty minutes into the ride, Charlie asked me, "How was your stay with Aunt Nina?"

"I learned a lot. I'm so grateful you introduced us."

Arriving at his camp, I told him, "I am going to ride the motorcycle home because I want to make sure I have some quick transportation around town."

He nodded. "I will follow you in my Jeep. I have a few things to do before we leave. You can come in if you want to."

"I am happy here. Thanks though." Waiting at the pier, I dipped my bare feet into the warm, brackish water.

Smaller fish nibbled on my toes in the murky waters just like my parents' camp. My mind drifted to the camp life, fishing with my papa--it wasn't a defined memory or a specific action, but we always

132

had a good time fishing even if we didn't catch anything. He always would clean the fish that we did catch and Mama would make the side items for dinner. My favorite was speckled trout or flounder--I can't decide between the two. Charlie broke my daydream and sat next to me.

He had his boots on and didn't dip his feet in the water. "Are you ready?"

Pulling my feet out of the water, I shook them to dry them off before slipping my shoes back on. I pressed my heel down into my Keds, holding the back of the shoe with my index finger to keep it from collapsing. Once both shoes were on, I said, "Yes. I am now ready."

We both got in our pirogues, and I followed him, assuming he knew how to get to my parents' camp. It was a long day and we wouldn't get home until dark. I was glad that Charlie was going with me, especially since I hadn't seen the dog Breeze in a while to direct me homeward. We arrived at a dock with a boat launch area. Coasting up, he tied his boat and, reaching for my boat, he pulled me in and tied my boat. As he darted off, I raised my palms up as if to ask, *What is going on?* But he was already gone. Moments later he came back with his Jeep and a small trailer. When he backed in to the boat launch ramp, the trailer dipped into the water.

"You are so efficient!" I said as I got out of my boat and went over to his boat to untie it and started to walk it over to the trailer.

Charlie met me. As he took the rope from my hand, our hands touched, our eyes met, and my face flushed. My heart fluttered a little. *What the hell is going on with me? Don't act a fool, Arielle!*

He smiled with a light chuckle at my bashfulness. After his boat was settled, I walked mine over to him. Charlie got both boats nestled on the trailer and secured with tie downs. We hopped into the Jeep, and he pulled off. I turned around to check the boats out the open back window. The gravel crunched loudly under the tires until we pulled out of the rock area onto the dirt road. I pulled my T-shirt over my mouth and nose so I wouldn't inhale the dust. Most of the roads this far into the swamp were not marked. We rode, listening to the whirl of the engine. I looked out the side window as we bounced around, wondering how long the ride was going to be and what I would fix for dinner. About twenty minutes later, we pulled up to my camp. A white dog was on the porch waiting to greet us.

I introduced them. "Charlie, this is Breeze." Breeze sat and lifted his paw to meet Charlie's hand and they shook.

"Hi, Breeze, it is a pleasure to meet you," Charlie said to Breeze, releasing his paw.

Charlie had work to do so he began to take the boats off the trailer and hang them on the hooks under the piling located under the camp to store them out of the way. I followed Breeze to see what he was up to. He took me to the place where Papa would fillet the fish we would catch. There were three fresh fish ready to be filleted. My mouth dropped. He sat and gave a smile and started panting.

"Charlie! Come see!" I turned to see him jogging over to me. When I turned back to point to the fish, Breeze was gone. "Look!" I pointed to the fish. "Breeze brought us dinner!"

Charlie's eyes narrowed as he looked at me. "The dog?"

"Yes."

Each deep in our own thoughts, we looked at the fish. Maybe it was poisoned? Could a demon take a form of Breeze to trick me? I didn't want to be duped into putting myself and Charlie in a bad position. I looked at Charlie as he looked at me and we shrugged.

"Do we eat it?" I asked.

"We are both hungry," he said.

I prayed over the fish out loud. "God, if You would please bless this food to nourish our bodies and keep us protected." I looked up at Charlie. He had his head bent down, praying along with me. I put my hand on his arm and said softly, "I think we are okay to eat this for dinner."

He raised his head. "Where the fillet tools?" I tugged the drawer on the wooden table open. The fillet knife was just where Papa left it. Gently I pulled it out of the drawer, holding it in my hands and taking a moment, releasing a long sigh.

Charlie put his hand on my shoulder and gave it a squeeze. The leather case covering the knife was stained and worn from usage. I could still see the letters 'PAPA' stamped into it. Handing it over to Charlie, I walked up to bring my bag and the other items Charlie brought along with him into the camp. I assumed we would crash here for the night.

Opening cabinets, I searched for a side dish. I found some brown rice that would be good enough. I laughed to myself as I prepared it. Mama always burnt about a third of the rice when she cooked it.

I peeked out the window to see if Charlie was still there. He was done with the fish and was wiping his brow with his arm. I found a pan and went to bring it down to him. He was just putting the leather cover over the cleaned knife and gently placing it back into the wooden table. After handing him the pan, I told him, "I found some rice and I hope you like brown because that is all we have."

"Sounds great." He followed me up the stairs and began rummaging in the cabinets for seasoning for the fish. Satisfied with what he found, he sprinkled some on the fish. The oil popped and sizzled as he placed the fish skin side down in the pan. The aroma of dinner filled the kitchen. I couldn't wait to sit down and dig in.

After setting the table, I sat to watch him move around the kitchen. He finished up the last touches of the fish with a dash of lemon juice in the pan that he found in the small refrigerator. "Dinner is ready." As we sat across from each other, he grabbed my hands and bowed his head starting the prayer. "God, bless us as we enjoy this food You have given to us. Keep watch over Arielle as she continues to learn Your gifts. Amen."

We let go of each other's hands, and I smiled and looked into his eyes. "And thank you for bringing Charlie into my path. Amen."

After I finished my plate, I leaned back and patted my stomach. I was full of a perfect meal.

"You are done, right?" he asked as he took the second piece of fish and polished off the rice. "This way we don't have any leftover food to deal with."

"Go for it. I can't eat another bite." Looking out the long rectangle window next to the table, I could see the sun was setting over the lake. "Are we staying here tonight? Right?"

"It's up to you," he replied between bites.

"I think we might as well just stay here for the night and go to the house tomorrow."

"Done."

Once we finished cleaning up in the kitchen, the sun was already asleep and the moon was halfway up.

"I don't know about you, but I am tired. Do you mind if I use the bathroom first?"

"I don't require a whole lot of sleep, so it doesn't really matter to me," Charlie said, looking around. "Do you want to show me where I am going to bunk before you crash though?"

"Of course, this way." I motioned for Charlie to follow me and showed him his room, which was my brother's room. I pointed in the bathroom as we started back down the narrow hallway. "Towels and stuff are in the cabinet over the toilet."

"Could you start a load of towels after you shower so I can have them dried before we leave tomorrow?" I asked Charlie as we stood closely in the hallway.

"Yeah, that is a good idea since y'all don't live here all the time. I can do it and I will put them in the dryer if I am still up."

"Perfect, thanks. Goodnight Charlie."

He softly pushed the strand of hair beginning to hang in front of my left eye. "Good night, Arielle." He slowly turned and headed back towards the kitchen.

I leaned against the hallway for a moment, wondering *What just happened? Nothing happened, Arielle.* I was in bed in no time, putting all the events in the hallway out of my mind. I fell asleep quickly and found myself submerged into another dream.

CHAPTER SIXTEEN
College In My Future

My dream was different because it was memory of a conversation I had with Papa before he died. I didn't even remember the memory until I saw a photo and asked him about it a few years ago when I was making a scrapbook for Mama's birthday. I was very young in the photo, probably about three or four years old. I was wearing a sleeveless white cotton dress with two medium-size brown buttons at the top. I handed a yellow flower to a boy in the photo. He had dark brown hair and was wearing blue jeans overalls with a white and red train hat.

"Papa, who is the boy in this photo?"

"That was your cousin Daniel. Your Grandpa Belland took that photo."

My grandpa, Martin Belland, was a professional photographer. He loved taking candid photographs. When we would visit during the summertime, the family reunion always entailed a group photo. It was a total drag, but looking back, he knew what he was doing capturing so many priceless memories. It's amazing what a photo can trigger in one's memory bank. And depending on whom you ask, you might even get a different version of the story. I was about sixteen when I asked Papa about this photo.

"You got in trouble in that photo. Do you remember any part of that?" he asked me.

I scrunched my lips to try to recall, but nothing was coming to my mind, "Nope."

"You told your older cousin Daniel to hold the flower so your Grandma Lilly could find him in heaven tomorrow. Daniel died in the middle of the night that next day. The family was up in arms over the whole thing."

Thinking about what he said, I thought, *How could you blame them?* How bizarre for a four-year-old to say such a tragic thing, and even worse that it happened!

"It was one of those random odd things. He stopped breathing in the middle of the night, and no one knew he was gone until the next morning. The doctors said he had a rare heart condition and that there was nothing we could have done for him," Papa explained, shaking his head with a deeply saddened frown.

The smell of coffee brewing caused me to stir as I lightly shook my head to dust away the memory. It was so nice Charlie was here making coffee before I even set foot out of bed; I could get used to this! That morning I told Charlie as we sipped our coffee, "It is really okay for you to go home. I know you have a business that you need to tend to. I am going to start college back up again in a week anyway. Not that I am trying to get rid of you, but reality is we have lives in different areas, and both have responsibilities to uphold." He stood at the kitchen counter as I slouched at the kitchen table hovering over my coffee mug.

He just smiled, saying, "I am right where I need to be. Like I told you before, Nick has the farm under control until the school field trips start rolling in. It really doesn't start rocking for another month anyway. You need to find your path, Arielle, and I am here if you need me. Even if it is only making you coffee in the morning."

"Very funny and totally awesome. I would never turn you away from making me coffee," I laughed. "I do need to get my classes registered. I promised my papa I would give college an honest try."

"Your papa sounded like a smart man."

"He was, but realistic too. Mark was not college material. He did one semester and had a GPA of .7 and his fate was sealed. My parents were not going to fund his "college" activities anymore.

They made him get a job, and shortly after that he met and married Nicole."

"College isn't for everyone, I agree. Just look at me. I have a successful business without that piece of paper," Charlie said. "I remember Mark during his college years before Nicole… He was a little wild, but he has always been that way. You know, you lived with him!"

"He was always getting into trouble as a kid. At least it wasn't anything illegal. Good thing Nicole was able to reel him in some. I don't really know what to do with my life, and I don't know if college can lead me where I need to be either. And I don't want to get a random job either." I sighed and ran my hands around the coffee mug, debating if I needed a second cup.

"Maybe take some fun classes. Don't you like art?"

"Yeah… I do like art. I could take some art classes and maybe an English class, but not math. I suck at math. How did you know I like art anyway?"

He laughed, putting his coffee mug down on the counter, leaning on his right arm, and crossing his leg at the ankle. "I pay attention. I remember you had a few things in the art shows in high school. How about I take you tomorrow to campus then you can sign up for a few classes?"

Sticking my tongue out at him, I finally agreed. "Fine! Mama will be happy I have a schedule." I took the last gulp of coffee from my mug and changed the subject. "So, do you have an idea when you are going back to the alligator farm?"

"How long do you want me to stay?" he asked.

"I don't really know, but it is great having someone make me coffee in the morning!" I said as I poured myself another.

"Speaking of coffee, I am sure you have nothing at home. We should to go to the grocery."

"If you are cooking then I am buying," I said, nodding my head with a big smile.

"Sounds like a deal. Let's head out and drop off your bike at the house and get some necessities, like coffee."

"You know me so well already."

Once we got back to the house with arms filled with brown paper grocery bags, he started making sandwiches for lunch. After I put away all the other items, I sat down with Papa's book at the kitchen table to soak up the information. We ate and I cleaned up the kitchen. Just as promised, he took me to campus and I signed up for two art classes, one English class, and one biology lecture. The days passed so fast as we didn't do much of anything but eat, talk, and walk the town. Everything was peaceful.

About a week later, one evening we settled in the family room with the TV on low. I asked, "Charlie, do you think maybe the demons are leaving me alone now since I am better equipped?" I counted on my fingers. "Since I have been home, we have had no encounters nor seen Miranda and no bad dreams either. And come to think of it, I have not seen Breeze since the night at my camp."

"Maybe... I hate to be a downer, but maybe they are waiting for something?" he suggested.

"I don't like that interpretation. Let's just pretend mine is the right one, okay?" I joked with him.

"Arielle, whatever makes you sleep better at night. But don't let your guard down."

Ringgg. I jumped up from the couch and dashed into the kitchen to answer the phone. "Hello?"

"Hi, sweetie! How are you holding up?"

"Hi, Mama! I'm good. I have missed you. Are you coming home finally?" I asked her.

"I am and I will tell you all about my trip when I get home. I will just take a cab from the airport. My flight comes in at 4 p.m. this Thursday; flight number is 1247. You want to write it down?"

"Are you sure you don't want me to pick you up? I can take the car, no problem."

"Nope, I am good. It is easier to take a cab. Will you call your brother and let him know I am coming home? I would like to have everyone over this weekend if they can come over," Mama told me.

"I will call him as soon as I get off the phone with you. I love you."

"I love you too, Arielle. See you Thursday!"

I couldn't hide the excitement about the news. I picked up the phone and dialed Mark immediately. "Mama is coming home!" I yelled over the phone at Mark while jumping up and down. "Y'all have to come over this weekend because she wants to see everyone."

"Let me make sure of the time with Nicole, but we will be there. Did she say she was bringing home presents?"

"No. She didn't say, but you know she always does." After I hung up the phone, I went back in the living room to ask Charlie, "You plan on staying over the weekend, right?"

Looking up from the TV news, he said, "I think this would be the perfect time for me to head home. I need to spend time getting a few things in order. Since I am already in town, I can pick up stuff and head back to the camp. And school is starting for you very soon."

"I might miss having you around."

"I know, and even worse, you are going to have to learn how to make coffee again, aren't you?" he joked. "Do you want me to take you to visit Father Beau tomorrow? You haven't made contact with him yet."

"I didn't call yet. I guess we could just show up and ask a few questions. That would probably be a good idea to meet him."

"Of course, it is a good idea. Those are the only kind I have."

"Oh Charlie," I said, rolling my eyes. "That is some goofy stuff like my papa would say."

*****

Packing my backpack with red powder, boogieman spray, and Papa's book, I finished my routine by checking for my necklace and tucking it under my peach blouse. I climbed into Charlie's Jeep, and he rounded the corner towards Father Beau's church. It was in a different parish, so we had a little while to travel. I was starting to feel a little sick bouncing around in that old Jeep when we finally arrived at our destination. I could hear the tires move from the sound of the uneven pavement to the crunch of the oyster shells that made up the parking lot. Once the Jeep came to a halt in a parking spot, we climbed out. Charlie just stood there looking at me.

"I guess I need to make the first move since this is the reason we are here," I said to him as I started walking to the church at the end of the parking lot area. "The church used to be a lot smaller before the last hurricane that flooded it, didn't it?"

Charlie said, "There were about five pine trees that fell onto it too. The amazing part was all the stained glass remained untouched. The church felt that was a sign and they should use the same windows in the next building. The church was rebuilt around these windows only on a larger scale." He pointed ahead of us. "See, there are six windows in the front by the altar area."

We could see three on each side of the middle of the church. The one on the far outside was the longest; the middle ones were a little smaller, and then the two center ones were the smallest in size. The windows depicted communion, prayer, scripture, baptism, the holy family, and the crucifixion with the empty tomb. The scenes had a lot of beautiful detail in them.

The sound of the crunching shells under our feet turned to the soft steps on the smooth, hot concrete. A high-pitched ringing sound pierced my ears as we neared the church. I glanced at Charlie. He didn't seem to hear anything or was just ignoring it. "Do you hear that?"

"No, hear what?"

"It's annoying… You don't hear it?" I shielded my ears as we stood neared the entrance. The sound was so loud I couldn't hear anything. Looking at Charlie, I could see his mouth was moving, but I couldn't hear anything he was saying because of the increasing sound. Giving a hard yank on the round metal door handle, I quickly entered. Once we were inside, I pushed the door shut with both palms and leaned against it. All I could hear was silence. I shook my head to cast out any sound that might be lingering in my ears.

"Are you all right now?" Charlie whispered.

"Yes, it is gone now. That was weird. I couldn't hear anything the closer we got to the church," I whispered back, gently rubbing my ears with my fingertips.

The church was extremely quiet; no one was in the sanctuary, but all the lights were on. I walked through the old pine pews, touching each one, dragging my hand across them as I passed, looking at the windows. The sunlight shone, creating brilliant colors that danced on the altar area. It almost looked like the orbs I saw with Aunt Nina, but these were different shapes of the cut glass. Making our way through the church to the side entrance, we found a door with a wooden sign pointing to the left and directing us to the office.

The door led us into a hallway. As the door creaked closed behind Charlie, our vision went pitch black. Dragging my hand on the wall as I walked, I felt for a light switch. Luckily Charlie flicked it on. Once my eyes adjusted to the light, I could see all the doors were closed in the hallway. Walking to the end, I knocked softly and opened the door. I peeked in. A priest and a woman sat at a small white round table. She was dressed in a powder blue suit with a cute matching hat. They both turned to look at me.

"Hello, I am sorry to interrupt, but I am searching for Father Beau."

The clean-shaven older man stood. He was very tall with sandy brown hair that contrasted his black clergy vest. He spoke as he extended his arm out, pointing to the table where they were sitting. "I am Father Beau. Would you like to join Ms. Marie and me for tea and scones?"

I stepped into the room with Charlie following me. "Oh, good, I have found you. Yes please, that sounds delightful." We pulled up two chairs and sat with Father Beau. Ms. Marie rose to retrieve more tea. I smiled nervously, waiting for our cups and for someone to break the ice.

Father Beau folded his hands and placed them on the table and asked, "What are your names? Are you here looking to get married at the church?"

I started, blushing deeply , "My name is Arielle Mathis. This is my, um, my..." I hadn't ever introduced Charlie before. I didn't know what he was to me, I settled on friend. He technically was my brother's friend first. "This is my friend, Charlie. No, we are not looking to get married," I said, glancing at Charlie to see if he was going to help me with my introduction of us. Charlie gave me a wink and didn't say anything.

Father Beau said, "Pleasure to meet you both. I heard a storm of angels marching towards the church when you arrived. Arielle, you must be carrying some very extraordinary gifts. What could I possibly do for you today?"

I looked towards Ms. Marie, who was pouring tea for us. I did not want to say anything to confirm or deny his statement, so I just shoved a scone in my mouth.

Father Beau, seeing my awkwardness, assured me, "You are in like company and need not worry about anything said in our presence. We are both were here to help."

After a gulp of warm green tea washed down the blueberry scone, I talked rapidly about Aunt Nina and my visit with her, then ended with the hunch that Miranda trying to harm me.

Father Beau nodded a lot while I talked, listening very intently to my story. Ms. Marie sat posed, holding her teacup. She smiled, giving me her full attention. She had lovely white gray hair that was fluffed around her rosy cheeks.

"I am here for more information. Do you think you can help me?" I asked.

"Most definitely I can assist you with information. Ms. Nina mentioned you would be visiting me," he said, rising. He returned with a large leather-bound book. He thumbed through it, licking his thumb occasionally to get the pages to open up. The pages were worn a darker tan color along the edges.

I leaned in with curiosity. Once he found the page he was seeking, he opened it wide and turned it around like a school teacher showing the pictures to the children. The two of us leaned over the table to look closer. Using his index finger, he pointed over the top of the book at a symbol. "Do you see this symbol?" Father Beau asked.

We both nodded. I said, "Yes, Father."

146

"This is what you are looking for when searching for evil demons," he said. The symbol was like the letter "C" only very wide and backwards with the points of the "C" close as if to almost closed up like the letter "O". "Do you see this other symbol?" It looked like a candy cane facing towards the left. "This is what you are looking for when searching for a safe haven. Have you ever noticed any of these symbols on buildings around town?" Father Beau asked as he rested the heavy book on the table and peered over the top. We could only see his eyes and nose over the height of the book.

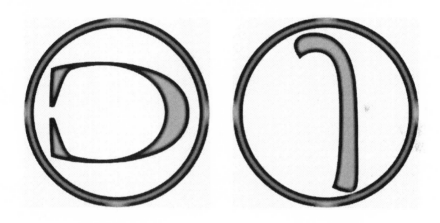

"I hadn't ever noticed them. There is a symbol on our home near the top peak, but it isn't either of those," I said. I described to him about the symbol. "It is like half of an "N" and half of a "D","," I tried to explain, using my hand to trace the letter in the air in front of us. A light trail of light escaped my pointer, finger leaving the suggestion of the symbol faded in our view. I quickly waved my hand over the area as the blue-traced symbol evaporated instantly. Snatching my hand back, I sat on both my hands bowing my head a little, not making eye contact with anyone. No one acted like they saw the light, I tried to act casual.

I peeked up to look at Father. He was turning the book around to himself and flipping through several pages. He showed us the pictures again. "Is this the symbol on your home?" he asked me with his pointer finger extended, pressing down on a different symbol.

I nodded with wide eyes. "Yes! That is it."

He explained, "That symbol is a mixture house. Both angels and demons enter the home. The house is never able to become a dwelling of just one or the other."

"So, is this not a safe place for me to stay anymore?" I asked.

"Well... the stronger you become, the less you will have to worry about. Keep your heart towards the white light with God and you will always prevail," Father told me. "How long have you been living in this house?"

"All of my life," I told him.

"You must have some strong angels watching over you, and God's hand is upon you. I think you might be all right. Just be aware of your situation so you can be careful," Father Beau told me.

Charlie said, "You can always stay with Mark or me."

"No. Your homes are both ways too far out, especially since I am going back to college now. I can't handle that kind of commute. There isn't enough coffee in the world to get me up early enough to make it to classes on time. I will pay attention to the buildings," I assured Charlie as I patted him on the arm. I asked Father, "What about being on the streets? Are there any safe areas other than just in these buildings?"

Placing the heavy book down on the coffee table, Father closed the cover as a few tiny, jagged bolts of blue light surged out of the pages and disappeared into a white smoke. His focus was on me, not the book as I tried to hide my surprise. He explained with a slight smile because my face was not hiding anything from him. "If there is a quadrant of buildings with the safe symbols and you are inside them, you are in a safe area. So, yes, even the streets can be a danger zone. Really, they are everywhere. Do you understand?"

I nodded while asking, "I was attacked in the swamp at Aunt Nina's house. There aren't any symbols in the swamp. How do I know I am in a dangerous place with no symbols to guide me?" Not giving him time to even answer, I squeezed my eyes closed, remembering, and asked, "And what was the high-pitched noise as I walked to the church?"

His eyes shimmered with love and excitement. "Over the centuries, the buildings have been labeled with these symbols, but it is a work in progress. The symbols are really portals, demons, and angels fighting to keep a balance of who enters our time line. Be aware of your locations and remember what contact so you will know for the next time. That is the only advice I can offer. You do have a gift. It is very rare that people can hear angels speaking. You can hear them in their native tongue." He said, "I will be very intrigued to learn more about your gifts."

I told him, "The sound was so overwhelming it was just noise, not a language. I have heard cries when souls are released, but this sound was something new. Can you hear them too? Can you see... um, odd things?" I asked with a side glance, wondering if I was the only one.

"Humans and angels are very different creatures. God never intended us to interact on a conscious level. Dreams and trance-like states are usually when people encounter angels and even demons. But you have something special to be able to connect with them without entering that subconscious realm. Work on learning how to communicate with your angels and maybe you can find the purpose that God has for you. I warn you, always make sure you ask for God's presence if you are communicating. You don't want demons to trick you with black magic."

"I understand. Aunt Nina told me very similar things, but you did tell me you can hear them. Can you?" I prodded.

"No, my child, I cannot directly hear them, but I could feel their vibrations when you came upon the church. I was gifted with the ability to read these historical books to pass on knowledge to chosen humans like yourself. I have learned the signs over the years. I can tell when you see things. Your face is an open book too."

"I know I can't hide much," I said with a slight eye roll. "Are there others like me out there?"

"Yes, there are, but unfortunately, most have turned to the demon side. Therefore, I urge you always center yourself, asking for God's white light to surround you. Evil is very tempting, and the flesh is weak. Evil will make you promises but be strong enough to see the deceit. Would you tell me a little more about the encounters you have had?"

"One that I will always remember is of my mama. She found a spot on her breast and went for a biopsy. She didn't tell us kids about it. Mama and Papa were still waiting for results before alarming the family." I remember the dream very well. "I was about ten years old and Jesus visited me. We were sitting together on a huge gray rock. I was like a small child sitting on her father's lap. He was wearing a white robe, and He looked like all the other pictures I have seen of Jesus, so I knew it was Him. Jesus told me when I woke
150

up, I was to tell my mama not to worry. He said it was not time for her to live with Him. I didn't know what He was talking about, but I did just as Jesus had instructed me and told her the message. She wrapped her arms around me and patted my hair. Papa came by, and she motioned for him to come close. She had me repeat the dream to him. He engulfed us both with a huge hug and held us for quite a while. I can still smell his cologne," I said, waving my hand under my nose to inhale the smell.

Father Beau said, "That is a lovely story and a brilliant example of how God meant for us to communicate with Him and our assigned angels. And you are every unique to have an experience with Jesus. Your angel might have taken the appearance of the "known" Jesus to comfort you in your dream, but maybe it was Jesus. I really don't know. Now that you are communicating outside of dreams, you are excelling at your gift. Your angels are trying to get your attention. Maybe one day you will be able to speak with them when fully conscious," he suggested.

I asked, "How can I see orbs? And hear angels speaking? I am just a young girl figuring out life. What makes me so special?"

Father Beau said, "Mary, the mother of Jesus, was just a young girl as well. But for some reason, God chose her for a very special task. Just like He has something very special for you to accomplish too. You just have to find out what it is. Don't ignore your gift. Embrace it and learn as much as you can to keep yourself safe. There is real danger with demons; I mean real danger as in fatal. I don't think God gave you these gifts just to have you waste them by getting yourself killed. Take your life and your gifts very seriously."

"Please don't compare me to the Blessed Mother. I am nothing compared to her," I said, shaking my head and saying, "No" sternly. "I just want to know what He wants from me so I can get on with my regular life," I said.

"That is a very good question, but I fear this is your new normal, and the sooner you come to terms with that, the sooner you can move forward. Why would you ever want to go back to being normal now that you know all these stunning gifts you have? Honestly, it is really between you and the heavenly Father to learn how to communicate with each other," Father said, "But you need to center yourself, pray, and obey the words He puts in your head."

Pray and obey; I repeated this in my head, slightly rolling my eyes and shaking my head again, not at all liking Father telling me this was my new normal. I leaned back and looked towards the ceiling, ruffling my hair and trying to get a grasp on everything.

"There will be times when you don't understand or want to do what God asks of you, just like Noah. You need to be strong and carry on," Father Beau said.

"To be frank with you, I am there now. I don't understand," I said in a sassy tone. Trying to not be rude and to show my appreciation, I toned it down, saying, "Thank you, Father and Ms. Marie, for your time, hospitality, and knowledge. We should get going." I gave a small side wave at Charlie.

"Anytime, child. Oh, and before you go, I have something for you," he said while he rose to leave the room. He came back, holding a small purple bag, and nodded towards me. Not sure what to do, I cupped my hands together as if to take communion. He dramatically placed the bag in the palms of my hands. I lifted the bag to my eyes to get a close look and pulled open the cinch top.

Looking back at Father, I gave him a puzzled look. "Thank you? It's a bag of old buttons and knick-knacks. What in the world is that for?" I asked him, unzipping the top of my backpack. I nestled the purple bag in the middle and zipped the backpack closed.

He nodded once, largely and with a great smile. "You are welcome. Hang onto that. You will want to use it on your adventure. Just remember, only use it to release the evil that is holding someone captive. Otherwise it will do you no good," he said as he folded his hand and bowed slightly towards me.

Both Charlie and I were now standing so we bowed back towards Father. "Thank you again for your time."

Silently exiting the church, we made our way to the parking lot. The sun was beaming through the long-extended branches on the nearby wisteria, which rustled as it moved fluently. *The angels must have moved on to somewhere else,* I thought to myself. Shifting gears, I asked Charlie, "Do you want to run your errands while we are out?"

"Sure, I might as well get the supplies I need for the farm." We spent the rest of the day running around town getting his items.

Thursday came bittersweet. Charlie was packing up his Jeep to head back to the alligator farm and Mama was coming home. I wasn't particularly good at saying goodbye. It always seems so awkward to tell someone goodbye. I never know exactly what to say. Charlie swung the last bag into the back of the Jeep and came around to the sidewalk. We stood facing each other as he rested both of his strong hands on my shoulder. I furrowed my brows and stuck out my bottom lip to show my annoyance. He let out a laugh, pulling me quickly in for a hug along with a short kiss on the top of my head and released me. I stood there with my hands wrapped around my arms. Pulling my right arm out, I gave a limp wave goodbye. He raised his arm out of the top of the Jeep and gave me a peace sign. I watched him drive down the street and a large sigh escaped. I guessed I would miss him.

CHAPTER SEVENTEEN

Making Amends

I stood in the foyer; the house was so still and quiet. I decided to go for a walk to get a few more groceries before Mama arrived. I tossed my backpack on and locked the front door. When I returned holding the two brown grocery bags, I thought, *There are plenty of days I don't want to have this gift. I don't want to have to talk to people, but I feel compelled to pass on these messages. Most of the time I have no idea what I am saying to people, but they take the pieces I share and place them in the broken parts of their hearts.* I placed one of the bags on the sidewalk and rested the other bag on my hip to open the front door, finding it was not locked!

The door swung wide as arms flew around me, almost knocking me down. Kisses flooded my cheeks repeatedly. "Arielle, I missed you so much!"

I laughed rubbing my cheeks with the back of my free hand. "I am so glad you are back!"

Mama took the bag from my arms as I stooped to grab the other bag on the sidewalk. I called to her as I walked in. "I have my schedule, and the weather is going to be getting cooler in the next few months, ya know."

"Finally! Sounds like we have plans for tomorrow. Did you clean out your closet to donate your older clothes?" she asked.

"I will start tonight."

She called to me later as she made dinner, "Arielle, I need to talk to you about some things now that I am home. I was going to wait and tell you and your brother at the same time, but I will tell him separately."

"Mama… what's going on?"

"I am okay now. Everything is going to be fine… I did go for the reunion this summer, but I also went for treatment."

"What!" I yelled, making her jump and drop the spoon she was using to stir. I picked up the spoon and walked to the sink to wash it off.

"I know you are upset I didn't tell you, but I didn't need you to worry. I was getting treatment, and everything is fine now," she told me calmly, still facing the stove.

"I can't believe… I can't believe… you didn't tell me. I could have gone with you. I could have helped you. I could have driven you places. What if you didn't recover? What if I wasn't there if you… if you," I fussed at her. I couldn't even finish my sentence.

"Arielle, calm down. Breathe," she said as she nonchalantly moved around the kitchen making dinner.

I shook my head in disbelief at her. "I don't know what to say."

"Say to me, 'Mama, I am glad you are home and doing great.' Now let's move on," she told me.

"What was the treatment for?"

"I have a blood disorder. It isn't exactly cancer."

"I am not hungry," I said. "I'm going to work on my closet."

"I didn't hide this from you to hurt you. You do know that, right?"

"I know, Mama. I am just overwhelmed," I said, defeated.

"I will make you a plate. You might want to eat after you go through your closet."

I went to my room to see what I could donate to make room for something new. Trying not to think about our conversation, I gave the clothes a hard push to one side and started from one end working my way through. Something caught my eye. I could see a symbol lightly carved into the plaster in my closet. How long had it been here? I know I am blond, but I am somewhat observant, I held the clothes back and traced my finger around the symbol. *Which one is this?* I thought as I raced over to my desk and dug around for a sketchpad to draw it. I dumped all the clothes on the floor to get a better view of the symbol. It was similar to a letter V and an upside-down letter V placed over it so they crisscrossed. I was on my knees staring at it and a purple color started to glow from the symbol. The color faded away as the symbol disappeared into the white plaster color when I heard Mama's voice.

"Are you making room for a few new clothes?"

I stood blocking the blank symbol with my body. "Yes, I am making some headway."

"Do you want some help?" she asked

I told her, "No thanks, I'm good."

"If you would like maybe we can go tomorrow to shop for some new things?"

"That would be nice." I carried several dozen items downstairs to donate to the women's shelter. I peeked in the kitchen to see what she made for dinner.

Mama motioned for me to come close. I fell into her inviting arms and she patted my hair. *I can't lose her too.* Fighting back the tears, I pulled away and examined the dinner plate she had made for me. I folded back the clear cling wrap and, jabbing my fork, I took a bite at the counter. "Mmm." I missed her cooking. She made one of my favorites called Shrimp Kac-Koo. I swirled the noodles around the white cream sauce and stabbed a pink shrimp on the fork. A smile formed as I pulled the utensil from my mouth and dived in for another bite.

Mama interrupted, "So what is going on with you and Charlie? Mark mentioned he saw him here a few times while I was gone."

I coughed a little. "Oh… we are friends. I don't know why Mark even mentioned it. It isn't any big deal." I moved to the table to finish my meal.

"Uh huh… I was reading the new *Time* magazine and thought the cover was very interesting." She walked over, plopping it down with a smack in front of me.

I smiled and shook my head from left to right a few times. The cover read, "Babies having babies." There was a teenager as pregnant as could be. She was turned sideways to really amplify her belly. I looked up at Mama with a half-smile to see if she was serious about this or not. Both her hands were on her hips with lips pursed. She was serious. I lifted both of my hands with palms up and the fork still in my right hand, saying, "I don't know what you are talking about."

She gave me a loud *sigh,* shaking her index finger towards me.

I said, "Mama, you don't have to worry. Nothing like that is going on. I promise!" Pointing with my left index finger towards my chest. "I made a promise to Papa to give college a real try… and ending up like this"--I pointed to the magazine cover--"isn't really giving it a good try, now is it?"

Her face softened and she smiled a little, "You sound a lot like him."

"I miss him."

"I do too, sweetie."

"I missed you too! I am so glad you are back and healthy. You are healthy, right?"

"I am, healthy, recharged, and ready if you need me for anything."

"I neeeed you to take me shopping!" When we stopped laughing, the house seemed so empty. No extra kids living with us and especially no Papa to always lighten up the mood. Minus the sadness in the house, things were going quite well for me. I continued with school, doing great in my classes, and keeping focused with little distractions. I continued giving out messages when spirits called upon me to give them. Miranda kept her distance. The nightmares and visiting demons ceased, causing my fears of going out at night to fade.

Charlie called a few times and we spoke on the phone. He was busy with his alligator farm. His cousin Nick had been sick with the flu so he was doing a lot of the work for the field trips. "I don't mind. I am not afraid of hard work at all."

"I still want to visit you and meet up with Aunt Nina. I have to tell her how quiet things have been."

"She would love a visit from you."

I suggested, "Maybe if you are free you could come in town for Halloween and we could go out on the town?"

"I will have to see about coming, but if that doesn't work out, maybe on Thanksgiving break I could pick you up from your parents' camp to come here and visit?"

"I have to talk to Mama about Thanksgiving. That is our annual beach vacation to Orange Beach. I might be able to do both. Let me know about Halloween."

"Okay, I will let you know as soon as I can. Take care, Arielle."

"Keep those alligators in check, Charlie! I will talk to you soon. Bye."

Laughing at me, he replied, "Bye, Arielle."

*****

I found Dixie at the campus library, "Hey, stranger! You want to go do lunch and catch up?"

"Sure, I could use a break. I will meet you over there in ten."

Finding a table off to the side near the large windows in the Union, I picked at the French fries and asked Dixie, "I am looking go to the quarter with Charlie for Halloween. If he can't go would you like to go with me?"

With a mouth full of cheeseburger, she said, "I have to see how much studying I have to do."

"Are you still mad at me after I blew up at you?" I asked, leaning in to try to make eye contact with her.

"A little... But I am really busy."

"I am sorry I was a turd. Will you forgive me and go with me?" I gave her my best puppy dog eyes.

"Okay, yes. I will go with you, but only if Charlie can't go. If he can go with you, I am out," she said, holding up her index finger with a glob of mustard on it. "And I accept your apology, but get it through your head, I am here to help you, but not if you are going to abuse me. Got it?"

"I understand, and I am really sorry. Thanks for going with me, only if Charlie can't." I emphasized with a sideward smile.

"Oh, Arielle, you are a mess."

"How are things with you and your man?"

"Arielle, you know I am so busy with school. We are not together right now. I don't have time for that."

I pointed over her left shoulder, "Are you sure he got the memo that y'all are not together?"

She turned to follow where my finger pointed. There was Ernie standing in the middle of a crowd of people walking around him as he stood watching her. Her head whipped around back towards me and she dropped her head back and sighed. "He just won't take a hint. I told him we are not getting back together."

"Dixie, he is walking over here. And it is more like a stalker than a boyfriend if he just stands there and doesn't talk to you anyway. Come on, he really likes you. Give him a break."

She picked up her book bag and left her half-eaten food, not even looking back. Ernie took her spot across from me. "Hey, Arielle," he said, very depressed and mopey.

"Hi, Ernie. I saw you over there being super creepy. Why are you doing that?"

"I can't help it, Arielle. She is all I ever think about. I can't eat, I can't sleep, I can't even go to class."

"Well, you better get your act together because if she ever does come back, you have to make something of yourself."

"You think she will come back?" he asked with hope glistening in his eyes.

"I don't know, Ernie, but I will try to talk to her again. Hang in there and get some rest. You look like crap."

"I know. I feel like crap too," he said and left me at the table alone to pick up our trash.

Leaving the campus, I continued walking around town and sketching down the symbols on the homes and businesses. Since Dixie was always so busy, I started doing more sketches, looking for a pattern or grouping of the symbols. I had a good collection and decided it was time I went to visit Father Beau and show him my "maps".

"He is not here. He has taken a group of adults on a mission trip and he will be back next week," Ms. Marie told me with her thick New Orleans accent suggesting she was from the sixth ward. Even though I grew up here, I don't have a strong accent. It was more of a Midwest sound. Maybe having Yankee parents was why I don't have the typical New Orleans accent. A few words do escape my mouth with the Southern twang.

"I have some new questions for Father Beau, and I would like to show him what I have been working on too. Can I leave my number for him to call when he returns?" I asked her.

"Of course, here, write your number on this." She handed me a tablet of 'while you were out' notes and a blue pen. "I will put it on his desk. How have you been?" Ms. Marie asked.

"I'm good now," I told her, glancing up from my scribbling. "Not much is going on with me. I am especially enjoying the quiet time. I am reading Papa's book. There are so many layers — voodoo, witchcraft, spirits and the church."

Ms. Marie said, "There are a lot of things evolving, the portals open and close so frequently now. I will make sure Father contacts you as soon as he returns."

"Thank you."

Leaving the church, I thought *I should really go see Aunt Nina again to tell her what I have learned and show her the book I am writing that is so parallel to Papa's book. I just have to convince Mama that I don't need to go on the family vacation for the whole Thanksgiving break.*

There was a note on the fridge that Mama wrote for me. "Charlie is not coming for Halloween." I called over to Dixie's house, and we decided to go to the street party in Jackson Square that Friday night. Settling on a costume idea, Mama put the finishing touches on my headband. I was going as a flapper girl. Mom sewed my dress with lines and lines of teal fringe. My headband had a few peacock feathers with the same teal color in it. I opted for the Mary Jane shoes instead of the heels. I didn't want to fall on the uneven brick sidewalks. Halloween night in New Orleans, was a huge street party with music and lot of partying.

That night I made my way over to Dixie's house. I pressed the doorbell and stood back, holding a sassy pose with my hand on my hip and one leg kicked out straight to the side. The door swung open and the light from the porch cast a light glow on her. She stood there in her pose with her face in a surprised look and eyes wide. She was Marilyn Monroe. Her white dress fit her body and made me jealous of her curves. Taking a few minutes to point out all the parts of each other's outfits we loved, we decided to walk to Jackson Square in case we had a drink while we were out. Locking arms, we giggled as we walked down the street. As we start to get closer to the French Quarter, the music became a little louder. The sounds of chatter and laughter rang out. You could feel the excitement in the air along with a slight coolness. A few people strolled by in costumes as we nudged each other and pointed out the different characters we liked. A rainbow bright girl skating on the sidewalk breezed by us.

"Blade?" I called out.

The girl screeched to a halt and spun around on her rollerblades to face us. She bounced off the curb and skated to us.

"Like totally rad," she said, then snapped her bubble gum. She stood about a foot taller than both of us with her skates on. Leaning down to our level, she gave me a squeeze and then Dixie too. Blade was her nickname in high school. She was one of the girls who had lived with us. She graduated and Mama and Papa helped her get into college. She came around for the first year and visited on holidays. After that first year, she took a job working at a roller-skating rink and as a professional roller derby girl. She didn't go back to college. From the looks of it, she was still skating around. We chatted about what she was up to, and she asked me how I had been. A few other girls on roller skates whizzed by, and Blade looked up and saw them too.

She said with excitement that matched the level of everyone around us, "This is going to be a fun evening. It was great seeing y'all, but I gotta jet!"

Dixie and I both called out as she sped off, "Bye!"

"I am ready for some fun. This is going to be a great night, isn't it?" I asked Dixie as we strolled down the street.

"So far so good!"

"It has been awhile since I have been out on the town," I admitted. "My fears have diminished about being out at night time. There has been no activity since the night at Aunt Nina's home. I have to fill you in on all the crazy stuff that happened when I was there."

"Well, let's go find someplace now and you can tell me," she suggested.

CHAPTER EIGHTEEN

Halloween

Dixie and I strolled Bourbon Street, taking in all the sounds and smells. The 'lucky dog' vendors were selling their hot dogs at a rapid speed. Sounds of the Michael Jackson hit "Thriller" poured out the bar as a group of zombies darted in the middle of the street starting their dance. Jumping off the curb, Dixie filed right in with a few other odd characters.

Clapping my hands to the beat, enjoying the dance, a cold breeze across my face, I followed the breeze as my eyes landed on a balcony one block away, lit by a single dim orange bulb. Squinting my eyes, I tried to focus on the dark balcony with several figures dressed in costumes. Brushing off the event, I turned back to the dancers.

As the song ended, Dixie tugged on my arm with a huge smile caught up in the excitement. "Let's get something to drink."

We slipped into one of the bars and stood at the counter. Getting an alcoholic beverage and being under twenty-one was not difficult in New Orleans. There a loophole in the law, so the bartenders could sell to someone as young as eighteen. But here was the catch--if you were under twenty-one, you couldn't legally drink it. This lets the bar owners off the hook and puts all the responsibility on the eighteen-to-twenty-year-olds.

It was common to see underage drinking. Another interesting thing is our open container law. You can drink on the streets, but no glass can be carried around. The marketers created some really cool souvenir plastic to-go cups. We crossed over, wandering down the street to get a curvy plastic hurricane cup filled with a red slushy drink. My cheeks flushed from the drink after one gulp.

As people asked us, "Where did you get those?" Dixie pointed and gave them directions. The cold breeze returned. This time it felt refreshing across my pink cheeks. Glancing down, I saw that my furry companion had returned.

I bent down and asked him, "When did you show up?" He gave me a slobbery lick on my cheek.

Dixie finished her directions and knelt next to Breeze. "What an adorable dog!"

"This is one of my spirit guides."

She wrapped her arm around his neck, giving him a little squeeze. When she stood up, he wandered off into the crowd. Watching him go, she asked, "Why is he here with us? And where is he going?"

"I have no idea, but I have an uneasy feeling about this." I tossed the rest of my drink in the nearest trash can; Dixie tossed her empty cup too.

"Come on, let's go dance." She grabbed my hand and pulled me into a club called the Cat's Meow. Music blared. "You Spin Me Round" by Dead or Alive--the place was spinning! I followed her to the center of the dance floor. She bounced around as her dress flowed around her body. I did my normal dance, a step to the left and a step to the right, repeat. Dixie grabbed a hold of my hands, pulling one towards her, making my flapper dress shimmy.

After she let go, I continued the shimmy and she squealed with delight, hopping around in a circle. I started to get the feeling I could let loose and have a good time as the song came to an end. A Cindi Lauper song came on the speaker next, the song "Time After Time" started. The dance floor turned into couples as guys started grabbing girls. Dixie was picked up right away. I scooted off the floor and stood on the edge near the dance floor's railing. Adjusting my headband, I patted down my dress. I felt a coldness on my exposed shoulders. Moving my head slightly to look behind me, I saw a white long skeleton's hand rested on my left shoulder. I glanced towards Dixie. She was locked in someone's arms.

My breath quickened as I leaned away and turned to face the same winged creature I saw last time I was with Dixie. It lunged to grab a hold of me with its other hands. I ducked down and slipped under the railing onto the dance floor, pushing my way towards Dixie. The creature let out a scream and everyone stopped and looked towards it. Everyone saw it; I wasn't the only one! I slapped my hand on Dixie's arm, pulling her away. She spun around and we bolted out of the door. The sky turned a dark red color, blocking out all the already dim stars, a black swirl developing directly above us. Dixie looked at me eyes wide with fear. I tried to hide mine from her. The random screams increased around us.

"I don't know what to do, Dixie."

"Do something!"

I joined my hands above my head with a clapping sound. A bolt of electric blue light shot out into the sky into the heavens. The light parted the swirling dark red sky. My body shook as I nervously dropped my hands to look at them. I glanced at Dixie; her eyes were so wide she looked like a cartoon character. I fanned my hands as little veins of the same blue light escaped from my palms.

"Holy crap, what is this?" Dixie said, bringing me back to the current situation. Looking over her shoulder, I saw the creature flying at full force straight towards us.

Without any thought, I brought my palms together and opened my fingers, pointing towards the bird. Dixie ducked quickly to the left as a single burst of light escaped my hands causing a direct hit. The bird burst into a red flame, then a single 'pow', gunshot sound rang out. A few gray feathers swirled down onto the pavement. A ripple effect of the crowd surrounding us let out a cheer.

I pulled out my pouch of powder from my cross-side purse and handed it to Dixie, telling her, "Toss it on anything that comes close to us."

We stood back to back in the middle of the street. Birds came diving down at us one after another. A bolt of light flashed out of me, and Dixie tossed powder so fast, creating a barrier. I could hear "Ooohs" and "Aaahs" sounding around us as the battle continued and we defended ourselves. I could feel the labored breath of Dixie as we leaned against each other as the terrifying birds began to retreat into the dark clouds in the night sky.

As the dust started to settle, the crowd erupted in approval! I was out of breath like I had just run a marathon. "They think we just put on a show for them." I reached for Dixie's hand and pulled it up towards the sky to end our battle finally, and a bolt of white light shot into the sky, forming a shower of glistening sparkles as it trickled back down towards earth.

She whispered to me, "I want to go home."

Still holding her hand, we walked fast into the crowd, waving as we made our exit. The crowd chattered around us, patting us on the shoulders, asking how we did that. We just waved and smiled, not stopping nor answering anyone. Linking arms, we weaved down the brick streets almost in a jog, leaving the commotion behind us. The streets were silent, and we made it back to her home safe. Fumbling with the key, she unlocked the front door and pushed me inside, closing the door, quietly leaning against it, and looking at me in silence for a minute or two. I didn't know what to say so I waited for her to speak first.

She asked in a whisper, "What the hell just happened out there?"

Tears brimmed on the edge of my eyes. "I really don't know. I have not ever shot blots of light out of my hands before."

"Holy moly, Arielle, holy moly!" She took my wrist and tugged on me to follow her.

We sat down in her room on the floor facing each other like we were about to play a board game. Her breathing shuddered and the tears began to flow. "I don't want to die, Arielle. The gravity of what happened is setting in. I'm not ready to let go of this world. I want to do so much--help people, marry, and have children!" She held her face in her hands asking, "What if I lost him?"

"You are pushing him away. Life is too short, Dixie." I pulled her hands away from her face so she could see my eyes. Her olive face was a little rosy and wet with tears. "Dixie, you can't live in fear. You can only live in the now. You go and get him. Make him part of the now," I said to her.

She turned to her clock. The short Mickey Mouse glove pointed to the nine and the long glove pointed to five. Nodding she picked up her phone next to her bed and turned to me. "Can I have a moment?"

I closed her bedroom door and crept to the kitchen for a snack. I sat at their table thinking, *Why did this happen? Everything was going so well.* I stuffed my face with Ruffle potato chips alternating with plain M&M's. I need to apply the advice I gave Dixie in my own life. Deep in thought, I mechanically handed a potato chip to the white dog next to me. His crunching brought me back to reality. "Hi there! Did you see everything that just happened out there?"

He looked up after eating the potato chip as if to say yes, or maybe he just wanted another chip. What the heck? I gave him another chip. Dixie came to the kitchen. I looked back at Breeze, but he was already gone. She leaned against the wall, playing with the magnets on the refrigerator. "Well?" I asked.

She turned towards me and a huge smile broke out on her face. "We are going out for a date tomorrow."

"Nothing like a fresh start," I responded.

She agreed with a nod and a huge smile.

I asked, "Do you want to talk about what happened tonight?"

She shook her head. "No, I think I am going to just keep it a memory. It is in the past and I am moving forward."

I said, "Okay. I am going to go home now."

"Do you want me to run you home in the car?"

"No, I will be all right. Thanks for the offer though." As I jogged home, a few more stray blue lights fell from my palms.

The house was empty when I climbed into bed. Mama must have gone out with some friends that evening because she wasn't in her room.

The dreary dreams started up again. I walked down a dark, damp hallway. I couldn't find the light switch as I ran my hand along the wall, trying to find my footing on the uneven ground. I heard winds rushing over my ears. I was getting an anxious feeling in the darkness but kept on stumbling to find a way out. Reaching a dead end, I felt around in the dark and realized it was a door. I gave the knob a twist. A beam of light shined from the room as the door creaked open. I peered inside; my brother sat in the middle of a white room on an old wooden chair with his face buried in his hands. My heart ached seeing his emotional pain. His elbows rested on his knees, and his shoulders slouched. The phone rang... His head dropped and shook slowly. I longed to know who he was talking to.

I woke up in a sweat. The digital clock flashed from 4:11 a.m. to 4:12 a.m., way too early to be awake. I didn't want to think about the dream, nor dissect it to figure out the meaning. I flopped back down in bed, rolling over and trying to get myself comfortable. Thankfully I did find sleep again with no more dreams. A distant sound woke me; I wondered what the sounds was... Oh, crap! That was the phone ringing... Why isn't Mama answering the phone? The answering machine must have picked up and the phone started ringing again. I pulled myself out of bed to answer it.

"Hello?" I croaked into the phone.

"Gris Gris got your mama."

"What did you say? Who is this?"

"Gris Gris got your mama."

"What? Hello?" I asked as I heard the click on the other end. The phone line was dead. I slammed the phone down on the cradle.

"Mama? Mama!" I called, running down the hall to her room. Frantically I flipped the light on. Her room was empty, and the bed was made. She wasn't in the bathroom. I darted down the staircase and looked in the kitchen, laundry room, and the living room. Everything appeared the same as last night. She was nowhere to be found. As a last attempt, I stepped out into our courtyard and looked around. The sun was peeking over the buildings as the birds chirped, looking for crumbs in the courtyard, but no Mama. *What do I do?*

"Mark, I don't know what to do. Mama is missing!" I told him, trying to keep the panic in my voice calm over the phone.

"Did you call the police?"

"No. I called you."

"Are you sure she is missing?"

"She wasn't home when I got in last night."

"What time did you get home?"

"I left Dixie's house around ten p.m. I guess."

"Are you sure she wasn't home last night?"

"I am sure she wasn't here when I got home, and she isn't here now. I got a creepy phone call this morning too."

"What do you mean a creepy phone call? What did they say exactly?"

"Gris gris got your mama," I told him.

"What the hell does that mean? Never mind. Call the police I am coming over. I will be there as soon as I can."

After about an hour of me pacing in the kitchen, I heard the front door open and Mark called for me. "Arielle?"

"I'm in here."

Sprinting, he ran smack into me at the doorway. "What is going on? Tell me everything. What is this gris gris crap you are mumbling about?"

"Something has happened to me." I wrapped my hands around my arms, not making eye contact with Mark as I began. "I met with a voodoo queen to try get some answers."

"Really, Arielle, what does this have to do with Mama? Why are you making this about you?" Mark asked as the annoyance in his voice increased.

"I think maybe her disappearance is my fault and my doing," I said.

"If this is your fault, you better figure out a way to fix this," he said in a stern voice as he grabbed a hold of my shoulder and gave me a shake to make me look up at him.

"I don't know if it is or not, but I need your help and understanding," I pleaded, looking him in the eyes so he could see my sincerity.

I reached for my necklace to check if it was still there. This seemed to become a habit for me to check for it. "I don't have time to explain everything to you, but I will once we locate Mama. I will try to give you the shortened version. Basically, I can communicate with people who have passed on, and angels visit me as well as demons. I think Miranda has captured Mama to lure me to her. Miranda either wants to suck all my powers and keep them for her own or she is going to try to convert me to help her with her evil ways." I spouted all this as quickly as possible, still holding onto the necklace.

Mark had a look of disbelief on his face, shaking his head barely as he tried to absorb everything I just threw at him. Mark knew I was always different but didn't really ask me or talk about it. After taking a minute to study his hand and pick at the cuticles that were jagged, he finally looked up at me and asked, "Okay, what do we do to find her?"

"I know where the home of Miranda is, but chances are she is not there having a nice cup of coffee and talking about the weather with Mama. I need to figure out where she is being held." I rubbed my forehead, trying to get the answer to pop into my mind.

"Why are we not going to the police?" Mark asked with his temper rising.

"Just shut up and trust me!" I yelled at Mark.

"What choice do I have anyway?" he fussed back at me, shoving the kitchen chair and making it rock forward, then landing all four legs, he started to pace.

"Stop yelling at me. We are not getting anywhere. Let me think for a minute." *Who can I trust that is close and might be able to guide me?* "Father Beau!" I exclaimed.

"Who is that?" Mark asked with a huge sigh as he stopped his pacing.

"He is a priest who is willing to help me and has a ton of information."

"How do you locate him, and do you need to bring anything?"

"Good idea. Let me grab Papa's book and my book that I am working on."

"Papa has a book? And you are writing a book too? What I was asking is what do we bring... like an offering?"

"We don't need an offering. I have met with Father Beau before. Mark, I have so much to tell you if you want to know about it, but that will have to wait."

"I'd rather be on a need-to-know basis with you. It is too much for me to understand your weirdness," he said, holding out his palm towards me like he was stopping traffic.

"I know, I know, and really some stuff isn't important. Let's go." With both books tucked in my backpack, I bustled out the door and quickly locked the deadbolt. He was gone by the time I turned around. As I stood wringing my hands, the car squealed around the corner as Mark pulled up onto the sidewalk and I jumped in.

I spouted off the last of the directions and to park at the space closest to the front door. My foot touched the ground before the car was fully stopped. Mark followed closely as I ran in the church down the hallway to Father Beau's office.

CHAPTER NINETEEN
The Chase

"Father Beau! Father Beau?" I called as I swung the door wide, storming in as if I owned the place. I darted down the hallway towards the offices, still calling for Father.

"Arielle, how lovely to see you again. I was planning on calling you next week now that I am back in town." He was sitting at the table with Ms. Marie. She wore a polyester peach suit; they had paperwork scattered in front of them. She turned and smiled at me, giving me a little fluttering wave with her fingers.

Ignoring everything, I pleaded, "I don't know where to find her. Can you help us? She is gone!"

"Slow down, child. Who is missing?"

"My mama."

Father stood and extended his hand to my brother. "Hello, I am Father Beau."

"Hello. I am Mark, Arielle's older brother. Arielle believes our mama has been missing since yesterday," he said, pointing towards me with an open hand.

A concerned frown crossed Father Beau's face. "Interesting. Do you know if she was missing from your home or while she was out?" he asked casually, motioning for us to sit.

Mark sat as I started pacing. "I have no idea. Maybe Miranda has taken her? Everything was so calm until I had an encounter Halloween night. I am seeing more of my powers and I don't know what to do with them." I glanced at Mark while I spoke. He remained calm and straight-faced. I wanted to tell Father Beau some other things troubling me, but that would wait until after we found Mama.
174

I perched myself of the edge of the seat next to Mark, trying to not get antsy. I began to bounce my right leg. "I am glad Aunt Nina told me to talk to Father Beau. You have all these useful books and so much information to share with me and I thank you for that, but I am here to find my mama. I am afraid she is in danger. Can you help me find her?"

"Let me see." Father Beau pressed his index finger to his lips and browsed along an impressive bookshelf. He chose an old book, setting it down on top of all the paperwork with a thud, and a bit of dust stirred from its landing. The image on the cover made me smile. It was good symbol. He unfolded the pages, revealing a map. He pointed out the pattern of the good areas and bad areas and mumbled to himself. There was one area shaped like a five-pointed star using homes as points. He pressed his index finger on one point. "Here, this is where I think Miranda will be found if she is not at her home. This is the oldest and still operating quarters for practicing voodoo queens and evil spirits and a highly active portal."

Mark and I looked at each other; it was right next to our home and close to the grammar school I went to. "I never knew all that evil was right at our doorstep," I said.

"Evil is all around us, child. You are just chosen to experience it in your life firsthand," Father Beau told me.

"Well, this evil has taken it too far now. Why are they messing with my family?"

"Arielle, evil knows exactly what to do to tug on your heart and crush your spirit," Father Beau said as he gently closed the book, but it still made another thud sound from the weight of the pages.

"They certainly have my attention now," I said, a little too sassy, flitting my finger up in the air.

Father Beau asked us as he extended his hands palms up, "Will you join me in prayer?" I was holding Father Beau and Mark's hands. My head bend down, and Father asked, "Gracious Father, please provide guidance, protection, and knowledge for Arielle and Mark."

We ended with all saying, "Amen." Short and sweet, my kind of prayer!

"Thank you, Father. I will be back. I want to show you my book I am working on and the correlations between mine and Papa's."

"Anytime, child. My door is always open to you and my library as well," he told me, pointing with an open palm to all the books lining the shelves.

It made me wonder, *Wouldn't he have lost all the books in the hurricane? That will be a question for another time.*

"Oh wait, what if Mama isn't at either place? Where do I go next?" I said, wringing my hands.

"Maybe it would be time to contact the police. If Miranda took her and is using her as bait, you will find your Mama. If not, then it must have been another unfortunate event and I would contact the police immediately."

"Okay, I understand. Thank you and goodbye." I waved to him and Ms. Marie as we left out the same door we came in.

With a clear head, I told Mark when we got back into his car, "Maybe you should go home to take care of your wife and son. I can manage without you."

"Like hell. Mama and you are my family too. I have to look over everyone now that Dad is gone."

I rolled my eyes and pushed my hair out of my face. "Fine, but don't get in my way. I need to go back home and get a few items in case I have an encounter with Miranda."

"I have no idea what you are rambling about, but I plan on parking the car there anyway. You can run in and get whatever you need before we head out."

Being both very strong-headed individuals, it was settled. We were off to Mama's house, then to look for Miranda to have a little conversation with her. Mark parked the car back at Mama's house. We cut through the courtyard and headed to the side door. Mark turned the key only to find the door was not locked or was even closed all the way. He gave the door a slight push and it creaked open. "Someone is in the house. Arielle, follow me in but stay downstairs till I make sure the coast is clear."

"Okay," I whispered as we both entered the house. I slowly closed the door behind me and crossed behind Mark to head to the kitchen. He stood at the bottom of the stairs and listened for any sounds upstairs. "Maybe we should call the police now?" I whispered from the kitchen. He waved his hand at me to tell me to shut up. Rolling my eyes, I went back into the kitchen.

I stayed in the kitchen while Mark went up the stairs to see who was in the house. I added to my backpack another bag of red powder and swung it onto my back, shifting my weight from one leg to the other, waiting to hear something... anything. I could hear the creak of the stairs while he walked up and the groan of the house as he walked around upstairs. My vision drifted to the kitchen window. There on the corner across the street was Miranda. She wore a long black dress and black lace veil. *There she is! Who could wear all that crap on a daily basis? It is like 90 degrees!?* Shaking my head and squinting my eyes in anger, I sprang into action.

I yelled, "Mark! Come quick! I see Miranda!" She moved towards the corner out of my sight. I yelled again, "Mark! Maaark!" With a quick click, I unlocked the front door, yanking it open. My tennis shoes slapped hard on the warm pavement. As I darted down the street, I grabbed for my necklace--still there. She was just out of sight and rounding the corner as I made it out of the door. A screech and a long honk filled my ears. I had darted out in front of a car. Twisting my head around, I waved at them as I kept running. I rounded the corner, nearly taking out an elderly man who was strolling with his cane. Making a football 360 turn, I was able to roll around him without knocking him down. My vision blurred. She was here and gone in a flash. There was no way she could walk that fast. This must be a trap. She appeared about three blocks head of me on the same side of the street, turning again, making the corner. I was better at swimming than running. I tried to pick up the pace to catch up to her as my backpack got heavier and my breath labored. She rounded the corner two blocks ahead of me. *You have got to be kidding me. I can't catch her! Keep going, Arielle. Reaching Miranda equals finding Mama.* Mark was nowhere to be found, but fear didn't consume me. I was determined to catch Miranda.

As I took the next corner, I realized I had followed her in a big circle, and we should be coming up to my house. Going around the last corner, I slowed tried to catch my breath as my chest moved rapidly. She was gone, as well as my familiar surroundings, the sky swirled above me in a purple haze. I walked briskly down the street glancing around. The houses lined the streets, leading me to a house at the dead end. The building stretched four stories with statues hanging off the pillars. The creatures had six eyes, four arms, and feathers. It was the same thing that had been attacking me. My heart thumped in my chest. *Was this a dream too? It can't be. I know I am awake. Right?*

I cautiously walked to the front door, keeping an eye on the creatures, waiting for them to leap to life. Atop the door a wooden banner with the with the name LaTour chiseled upon it. I looked up at the bird statues. They held shapes in their clawed skeleton hands. The symbols they held were like half of an "N" and half of a "D" just like was on our house. It was a mixed house where angels and demons could enter; at least I could call upon some help. I kept my eyes open and prayed, *God, please send Jacob, along with all your mightiest angels to come protect me!* I nodded, saying loudly, "Amen!"

Grasping the door-knocker, I dropped it, making a loud clank just as Mark hollered, "Stooop!" It was too late. The bottom of the doormat fell out as I twisted around, catching a glimpse of Mark running towards me. His arm was stretched, and eyes filled with fear. I slid feet first down a dark, slimy shoot as the door slapped shut, locking out the daylight.

I landed hard on my butt in full darkness. Feeling the damp, uneven walls, I walked down a hallway to a door. I thought I heard voices, but I couldn't tell where the sounds were coming from. The door was actually quiet as I opened it. Finally, something was in my favor. Peering out to the left and then the right, I saw something white and jumped back, then peeked out again. It was Breeze. Swinging the door all the way open, I squatted down and gave him a good scratch under his ears with both of my hands. His white fur was now dirty from the grossness covering my hands from feeling around in the dark. Breeze gave me a lick on the cheek. I knelt on both knees and opened my backpack to pull out the purple bag and put it in my pocket. I filled my other pocket on my denim shorts with the crushed red clay. I placed the backpack on my shoulders. "Now what?"

CHAPTER TWENTY

The Battle

"I am so happy to see you!" I told him quietly. "Not that you could do much for me, but at least I am not totally alone." I patted him on the head, asking in a whisper, "Where should we go now?"

He sat down and panted, just looking at me.

"You have no clue either, do you?"

It looked like he gave me a quick nod as if to say *yes. Am I imagining this white dog is nodding at me?* I looked down both hallways and chose to go to the left. The hallway ended, forcing me left till I was back where we started. There were no doors. *Maybe I missed it?* Surely Breeze would have alerted me if I missed my opportunity. I turned back to consult with him; he was gone.

I walked around the hallway again. This time I ran my hand and whole arm along the wall to see if I could feel where a door might be hidden. There was a bump in the wall. I stopped and started to feel all around the area, pressing with my palms in different areas. Passing through the hallway again, I noticed some mold in the ceiling corners.

Ew, was that there before?

As I looped again, the mold was now consuming the wall and filling in towards me. I found the part in the wall that didn't feel flush. Frantically I dug my fingers in to release the part of the wall to escape. Taking a quick second to look back again, the mold had turned into black beetle bugs. The sound of millions of bugs scurrying around, *ugh!* At least they didn't fly.

Just then one flew and landed in my hair and I let out a screech I just couldn't contain. "EEEEK!"

I don't like bugs, and I really hate cockroaches. Yanking even harder, something finally started to happen. The wall expanded as a dingy white door frame appeared to me with a door and handle. I opened it, entering quickly and slamming the door, leaving the bugs behind me. I shuddered and flapped my arms to knock off any bugs still lingering. There weren't any, but I didn't want to chance it.

Taking a deep breath, I pepped myself up. *Relax a little. You are starting to figure things out. You may be clumsy and blond, but you're no dummy! See, you got away from those nasty bugs. When you find Miranda, you ask her what's her problem? And why do you have so many bugs in your house? It's just gross.*

The door had opened into to a very large room. All the drapes were drawn and it was dark in the room. Still leaning against the door frame, I glanced around and noticed two fireplaces across from each other. Low flames flickered in each one.

This is really odd--for this time of year to have a fireplace going.

The room was unusually cold even with the fires crackling as if they were speaking to each other and flickering at me. I exhaled, viewing the fog of my breath forming from my mouth. It took a life of its own and swirled out of my mouth, moving across the room, like it had a power of its own. I watched the new development of moving fog I created. It took the shape of an animal. A small lion formed in front of me, running in slow motion. The lion was the size of a small kitten, but had all the features of an adult lion. I reached out to touch it as it faded. I drew another breath to see what would come out next. Choking before I blew out my breath, I saw Miranda appear in my view, watching me in silence. I sputtered and a few small puffs of breath came out--tiny mice dancing around in front of me, between us.

I could feel the temperature changing around me, a blast of warm air, then freezing cold air swirled around me followed with scorching hot air across my face, making me squint from the heat. I didn't realize what the temperature changes meant because I couldn't see them yet, but it was angels and demons circling around me, and they were facing off against each other and preparing for a battle that was about to happen. Good versus evil were standing face to face in this odd place. I straightened up my body and tensed, with wide eyes watching Miranda. She locked eyes with me. She glided swiftly as if a nun was coming to slap my knuckles for something I had done wrong, arms folded across her body. As she moved, they unfolded and spread wider. She appeared larger as I shrank in size. I knew in reality, we were about three inches different in height, but I was feeling like she was five inches taller than I and growing.

I was starting to panic. I thought about Aunt Nina and the things she told me. I clutched my necklace; I could feel warmth around me increasing, not too hot, but warm feeling like being surrounded by many who love me. Now I was growing in size and Miranda was becoming smaller. When there was a shot of cold air, it would puff up my hair around my face. Each time the frigid air touched me, I saw flashes of images, faces formed with each of the bursts of freezing air. Fog engulfed the faces as they whizzed by me. Some were animals and birds. Some were unknown to me, but they all were terrifying.

The faces with sharp, pointy teeth chomping at me pushed my confidence as fear took over my mind. Each time Miranda appeared to be larger than me. I understood how emotions could control my perception. This world was about all the senses, not just what you see with your eyes, but feelings, smell, seeing, hearing, and even tasting. Each demon would "show" me something that I feared would knock me down.

I could taste blood, feel pain, smell burning, and see their awful faces. They were all made of the same fog I played with when I first came into this room. Dodging past one of the demons, I scurried over to the wall. I could feel something behind me radiating. Turning around, I traced the image on the wall with my fingertip, the symbols for both angels and demons. It began to glow a deep red color and pulsed as I backed away from it into the middle of the

182

room. I stumbled upon a portal with a battle emerging, with Miranda and I being the only humans.

I called aloud, spinning around with my arms raised toward the ceiling. "Okay, Papa, you said I was the one with strength. Let's see it happen now or never!"

Dropping my gaze and arms, my eyes met with Miranda's. We were about an arm's length away from each other in the middle of the room.

I spoke to her in a whisper. "What do you want from me?"

She hissed back, "Your soul."

"You are not going to get it. It is mine!" I shouted back at her shoving her a little.

Angels and spirits semi-circled around me, chanting words. I did not understand the language they spoke, but it had a rhythm like a hymn. Demons echoed laughter and chants back at the angels and spirits as they swirled behind Miranda each one uniquely terrifying. They slowly morphed into huge bodies. Some with armor and weapons; others had wings. They glowed dark colors.

I asked Miranda, "Don't you know that evil doesn't ever win?"

I could see a smirk form under the veil, and her eyes narrowed. "There is a time and place for every side to win," she said.

I didn't like that answer from her; some doubt started to creep in, but I shook it off, keeping my mind confident.

Miranda began to try to sway me over to the dark side. "There are many riches I can give you if you would follow me. You could live forever and never age."

"Impossible, you can't offer those things. All things must die according to God."

"You don't have to follow God and all His petty rules if you don't want to. I can offer you much more than He can." She curled her finger, playing with the edge of her veil.

"No!" I yelled towards her and flung my arms up, causing a blast of air to whip her veil around.

"If you won't join us then I am taking your soul. Replenish my strength. When I take all your gifts, you will be nothing. I am giving you one more chance before I demolish you." She reached out to me; her long black nails circled up. A breath of fog passed through the holes from the veil. Pausing for a few seconds, they joined together, creating the head of a hog with fangs and tusks. It snorted, squealing loudly and charging at me.

I swished my hand at the hog as it lunged at me. I dropped to the left to duck just as it missed coming in contact with me. I didn't know if it could truly harm me, but I didn't want to find out either. Scrambling off the ground I kept my eyes fixed on Miranda to see what she would do next.

Stretching her arms towards the ceiling and flinging her arms towards the ground, the long black lace cloak morphed into black wings. Her veil dropped and floated to the wood floor as her skin bubbled up and feathers dripped out of her face covering as if she was transforming into one of those ugly birds.

I looked around me for help from the spirits, trying to hide my fear as I backed away from Miranda. *I couldn't transform into anything. How could I fight this creature?* My angels flew in circles surround me, blocking Miranda from my view. Their white shimmering wing feathers blinded me as one landed on my left side and one on my right. Each one plucked several of their feathers, jamming them into my shoulder blades. "Ouch!" The pierce of my skin caused a trickle of the blood under my shirt, but the pain wasn't crippling. It was almost exhilarating. I glanced at my bitty "wings" given to me by God's angels.

My wings grew as angels two at a time flocked around me repeating the motion. A blur of white swirled around me and I couldn't see anything other than feathers passing rapidly around my body. Seconds later, all the angels, spirits, and demons fell silent and faded from my gaze, I examined myself in one of mirrors next to the symbols on the wall. I stood flat-footed, twisting and pulling my shoulder in to get a better look at my white glistening wings. They were drawn as I spread them to see the span. I couldn't see the tips in the mirror. As I closed them, Miranda's new bird form appeared in the background reflection.

Her body hunched over with her arms bowed out and her "claws" were growing longer. Before she could lunge at me, I jumped up in the air, spinning around, testing out my new wings catching a little wind, then I landed facing her. She immediately dove towards me. Squatting down, I pushed off the earth with all my might, flying straight up. She missed me and bounced into the wall, vibrating the mirror and causing a motion that rippled like water. *Could that be a portal?*

Turning my head away from the mirror demons, spirits and angels filled the room. The demons took their full natural form, terrifying me more, where the white spirits took forms of animals. All that comforted me, and the angels looked like all the traditional angels from paintings. Waiting for a cue from someone, I used my wings to tread in the air, slowing rotating taking in everything. Flying was amazing and effortless, not like the energy needed to tread water. It felt natural as walking. Breeze appeared below me. I knew now from the look in his eyes, Breeze was my dad; he was here to help me fight this battle. I bowed to him, still in the air, to thank him for all he had done for me and continued to do for me.

I raised my right arm towards the heavens and called upon God, "Lead us into this battle!" A white bolt of light escaped from my fist. The roof of the building blew off. We were exposed to a midnight blue starry sky. My blue orb and all the other orbs swirled; dark bubbling clouds formed on Miranda's side. We were equally matched, quantity for quantity, for this battle. Miranda threw her head back and let out a piercing scream. Still in bird form, she spread her cloak. It transformed into a second set of raven wings. Becoming airborne, she locked eyes with me, angrily flapping her wings, picking up speed straight at me.

I didn't know how to fight her. I really only knew how to protect myself. I spun in a whirling motion with my wings wrapped around me flying higher and higher. I dropped some red powder clay on her as she whizzed by me. It touched her wings, catching them on fire and burning them off, leaving a spot missing of feathers.

If I could get her wings off, just maybe I could defeat her?

I took another handful of red dust out of my pocket, tossing as much as I could. With each contact, she paused to regain her balance. This gave me a chance to toss more at her. She tried to slap out the fire with her leather claws. With so much of my special clay hitting her, she turned into a ball of fire. Miranda, now on the ground shook like a dog tossing off the flaming feathers, I hovered above her, holding the powered clay and waiting for my next move. I dodged a few of the feathers. They flew like shooting stars. Consumed with my tasks, I didn't realize I was in her territory.

I began to feel pain, ice cold, sorrow, hate, and hunger. I couldn't concentrate on Miranda because of the sensory overload. The demons were all around me filling my ears with evil laugher and pushing me up into the portal away from my angels. My wings were not working. I started to fall from the sky. My strength was being sucked out of me as I started to black out, shaking my head, trying to hold on to consciousness. My fall sped up.

Rapidly blinking my eyes, I could see white streaks whizzing around me, the colored orbs pulsed like a strobe light. As the horror faded and my joy came back and I realized I was not going to black out. As my anger grew, my strength returned. I would not be defeated, and I could defeat all the evil!

The demons attempted to pluck their feathers, piercing them into Miranda to create wings, but it did not work. Each feather fell
186

out of her skin and floated to the floor, becoming useless. As she morphed, the bird form faded, her eyes merged back to two, her two extra arms disappeared, her veil was gone, but she still had her long flowing lace cloak on. That must be her protective enchantment and I needed to get that off of her but keep mine intact.

I realized I wasn't going to just protect myself anymore, I needed to fight back to win this battle. Flying up high to pick up speed, I aligned myself to tackle Miranda. I could hear the screams of the demons when I blew past them towards Miranda. I didn't look at any of them; my eyes were fixed on my goal. She didn't know I was above her and quickly approaching. She caught on seconds before I made contact as she shielded her face with her arms, not realizing what I aimed for.

I grabbed a hold of her lace cloak, ripping it off her neck as I sped off towards the sky. Her screams sounded like I took off a layer of her skin as she dropped to the floor on her knees, frantically searching for her cloak. I tied her cloak around my waist because I didn't have my backpack with me. Her face snapped up, glaring at me, anger burning in her eyes as they turned blood red. She screamed a fog of breath at me. It transformed into daggers flying towards me. I dogged them, but they circled back towards me again. Realizing I couldn't out fly them, I used my wings to shield myself. The daggers pierced into the feathers burning a section of them off. Thankfully, I could still fly with what I had left. The angels rallied around me to try to replace my feathers with their own. As soon as they were replaced, Miranda tossed out another round of daggers and the whole charade started over again. This wasn't going to make us win. Eventually all the angels would be out of feathers and none of us would be able to fly.

How am I going to win this battle? Help me please! I want to win, but not just for myself, for Miranda. How can I help her come back to You?

The purple bag of buttons! Father Beau had told me, *use them and you will know when the time is right.*

Scanning the area around in the room, I located my backpack I'd dropped near one of the mirrors. She let out another round of daggers. I flew by the demons and spirits that were battling one on one. Landing, I could feel the heat from the daggers burning off my feathers as they made contact. I unzipped the bag and pulled out the purple bag. Inside was a small glass mason jar. I took a deep breath, holding the clear jar with both hands and wondered what to do next. I dodged a set of daggers and flew above Miranda, jolting to a stop. I exhaled a prayer onto the lid. The jar floated from my hands while I hovered above her. The gold lid glistened and began to breathe like it had life inside the jar. The last set of daggers made contact again and I dropped a little from another big loss of feathers. The demons continued fighting with the angels and spirits nearby. It was just Miranda and me. I was putting my life on the line for hers. I knew there must be a good woman inside; she was just taken over by evil.

My breath came out and wrapped around the whole jar with a fog likeness. The jar expanded then exploded, forcing me back from the explosion. The sound was so loud everyone stopped the fighting and turned to look. The simple buttons spilled out and gravity took over as they fell to the earth where Miranda was. The bits of glass turned into fire and looked like burning pieces of paper drifting down to the earth so very slowly. As the buttons fell, they turned into bright-colored orbs. They sprinkled in different sizes and landed on Miranda. Her skin lit up like the colors of the orbs. She shone so bright I had to squint to watch.

Surrounding us, the orbs landed, forming circle patterns. They illuminated the area and glowed so brightly. Shielding my eyes, I peeked at them. It was so beautiful I wanted to see it full-faced, but its splendor was so great I just couldn't take it all in. Miranda fell from her knees flat onto the ground. All the colors started to blend together so she was entirely covered, then the colors faded and all became white. So white it was blinding, I turned my back using my wings to shield myself from the brightness.

I didn't even realize I was descending to the ground and my feathers were starting to fall out. Softly my feet touched the ground as I went down on one knee and hunched over, feeling the warmth from the overpowering lights. The demons started to fade in silence. The angels and spirits disappeared singing hallelujah. I didn't want them to go. I reached out for them, peeking over my arms, but they dissipated like the sunlight hitting fog in the morning.

"Don't leave me!" I cried out to them.

I watched as the roof began to reconstruct itself back onto the building. The orbs flickered and blinked out as the bright lights that engulfed Miranda faded away too. It was dim in the room. The only light was the flicker from the two fireplaces again.

As I turned around I saw she was still on the ground. Her face was to the ground and her arms around her head. She was lying down on her side, and part of her leg was curled under herself. I didn't know what to expect so I slowly walked up to her, untying the cloak that was still around my waist. She let out a groan and tried to sit up but collapsed. I knelt next to her, as she looked at me, trying to focus. She didn't know who I was. I needed to know where my mother was, and she had no clue who I was. I was certain she wouldn't know where she hid my mother either! She was not strong enough to stand so I sat next to her.

She started to come to and asked. "Where is my cloak?"

I held it out for her to see it and handed it to her. "I have it here."

Anger crossed her face as she snatched it from my hands, "Give it to me!"

"Here take it," I told her defensively. "I am here to help you," I said with my hands raised palm side up.

"The demons are going to get me," she said quickly wrapping her cloak around her shoulders and scanning the area.

"They already did, Ms. LaTour. I am looking for my mama. Do you remember anything?"

She shook her head as she placed her face in her hand and scratched her forehead with her long fingernail. She was still trying to sort out the present let alone the past. Time would help with her memory. We just sat there for quite some time in silence. I could see the flames starting to die down in the fireplace.

I asked, "Do you want to try to stand up?"

Together we got her to her feet and shuffled towards the door. This was the same door I came in with the never-ending hallway. I wasn't about to argue with her about where we were going, I just helped her along. Opening the door, it was a beautifully decorated home with lots of fancy things. A stark white bear rug on the floor, huge paintings hung on the wall. There were decorative lamps, and very ornate furniture was placed around the room. I helped Miranda to the closest chair. It was a fleur-de-lis pattern in black and gold. The fleur-de-lis looked just like the one on my necklace.

After she sat, I knelt next to her as I drew my hand up to make sure the pendant was still there and it was. Thanks goodness. It was becoming like a security blanket even though it doesn't work on all demons and evil spirits. It is good to have to keep my strength and confidence up.

She noticed me holding the pendant and commanded, "Let me see what you are holding."

I wanted to act nonchalant about it, so I leaned in and let her touch it and look closely at it. I was waiting for her to rip it from my neck and push me down like this was all an act.

"It is quite lovely," she calmly said, "It reminds me of an old friend, Nina."

My wide eyes gave it away. I can't hold secrets or lie to save my life. She knew I knew Aunt Nina. I waited for a drill of questions, but she left it alone.

"Everything is so hazy," she told me as she rubbed her head. "I do not remember anything. We will have tea and talk about this on another date."

I started to object. "No! This can't wait! I need you to tell me where my…"

The double door across from where we entered opened and a man called out, "Miranda! Where have you been?" as he ran to her. He grabbed a hold of her hand and knelt at her side. I slowly rose and back away from them as I watched them. He asked her a million questions. He was talking so fast with his thick accent you would think it was a foreign language coming out of his mouth.

She shushed him and placed her index finger over his mouth to calm his chatter. She said, "I don't know what happened or where I was, but I am home and safe now, with my new friend."

Her arm extended to point to me. I didn't have that cold, eerie feeling like before with Miranda; whatever had a hold of her was gone. I didn't understand how the buttons could have that much power.

"With all due respect, I am not leaving until I get some answers from you," I said forcefully to Miranda.

"Child, you must be mistaken talking to us that way," Big E scoffed as he rose, crossing his arms across his broad chest. "Who are your kin?" he asked, leaning towards me with his eyebrows furrowed.

"I am the daughter of Mr. and Mrs. Mathis."

"I would think your Father would have taught you more manners than this," he scolded me.

"What he did teach me is to stand up for myself and what I believe in," I retorted, standing tall and crossing my arms across my chest, mimicking him.

"Please, stop all of this," Miranda blurted out, holding her arms out to separate us. "She must be in need of my help to be so persistent. Would you give us a moment, honey?"

"Nobody disrespects me, especially in my own house. Remember that," he said as he shook his finger in my face and walking out, slamming the large wooden door.

She patted the chair next to her. "Come here, child. Let me read your heart." She reached out for my hand as I approached.

I gave her my hand and sat as she asked me to. She turned my palm up and gazed into it. I listened to her softly speaking in a flowing Creole language that turned into a chant, over my palm. She rocked slowly and closed her eyes. Her chant became louder and her voice turned deep. "Gris, gris is going to get you."

I yanked my hand away from her and scrambled to my feet as I held my hand to my chest to keep it away from her. "It was you calling me and harassing me all along! I should have known you were behind everything evil and bad. Where is my mama! What have you done to her?"

Her eyes popped open, and she looked with surprise. "I remember now." Her look turned to terrified as she shook her head.

"What is it? What did you see? Where is she?" I yelled at her.

"I am so sorry. I didn't know I was a pawn. I didn't mean to hurt anyone," she explained.

"Where the hell is she? What have you done?" I pleaded. "Just tell me!"

"If she is still with us, I know where she is."

CHAPTER TWENTY-ONE

The Search

"Well, get the hell up and take me there right now. You are going to fix this. You are going to make everything right!" I grabbed her arm, yanked her to her feet and pulled her to the doors. She followed behind me like a puppy dog. Big E stood outside the double doors waiting for us. Seeing me pulling on Miranda, he lunged to grab a hold of me. I held up my free hand as a bolt released from my palm. He fell to the floor. Miranda tried to pull away from me to go towards Big E.

"Don't even think about it," I said, turning to face her. "He is fine, just stunned a little. Come on and take me to my mama right now and no one will get hurt."

She nodded and glanced at Big E slumped over on the floor, "She is in the tunnels under the city."

"What tunnels? The city floods even with a light rain. How are there tunnels? Wouldn't they just fill up with water?"

A rumble of thunder echoed around the house. It had not rained in about a week and we were due for an afternoon shower. Miranda pulled her arm free and looked me square in the eyes. "We need to hurry before the rains start." She hiked up her long flowing dress and started to run to the front door.

I ran right behind her, looking around and asking, "What direction? Where are we exactly anyway?"

"We are at my home, the Old Beauregard-Keyes House." She started off down Chartres Street, heading towards St. Phillip Street. "The main gatherings would be under Bourbon Street. We should go above ground until we get to Lafitte's Blacksmith Shop on Bourbon Street. We can enter the tunnels from there."

"How have I never known about the tunnels when I have lived here all my life?" I asked, keeping my job level with hers.

"All of the entrances are very secretive. You must know exactly where to enter and, more importantly, how to open the gates to get in. I hope you are ready for some interesting sights." She picked up the pace with her cloak billowing behind her as the cold rain started to plat on the hot concrete, creating a mist around our feet.

"Ms. LaTour, all I care about is getting my mama back safe," I called out behind her as I started to jog and pass her up, stomping hard on the puddles starting to form on the uneven brick sidewalks.

"Turn left on to Bourbon Street and we will be there," she puffed behind me. "Follow my lead," she said to me. I paused, my wet hair plastered to the sides of my face, watching her glide past me into the side of the building. Huge banana leaves covered the side walkway. She gently pulled them back to expose a dark red brick wall.

Turning around to make sure I was watching her, she put her hand in her front breast pocket and pulled out a metal coin. She wedged the coin into the grout line and slapped her palm flat, pushing the coin between the bricks. When she removed her hand, the coin was gone. The grout line started to glow a deep purple color. The color traced up the bricks and over, creating a door frame. She tapped the inner bricks and they waved like they were made of water.

Miranda reached back, grabbed my wrist, and pulled me forward as she walked through the bricks, taking me with her. It took about fifteen second for my eyes to adjust to the darkness. A small cough escaped as the smell of mold hit me.

Miranda opened her palm with her finger curled like she was holding a ball. The empty area in her palm glowed orange, creating light, showcasing a set of cement and brick stairs leading down. I mimicked Miranda and created my own light source that shone blue, just like my orb.

"We need to get moving before the storm fills in the tunnels," Miranda said while she motioned for me to start walking down the stairs.

I was scared, but my fear of not seeing Mama again gave me the courage to take the first step. I tried to walk quickly and carefully down the slippery steps. Once I reached the bottom, my ankles were completely submerged in water. I told myself, *Don't think about snakes or gators, just focus on Mama.*

"Ahead, veer to the left and there should be an opening up ahead. Take the tunnel to the left after the opening." I nodded and sloshed along in the water. Taking the left tunnel, the water was now up to my knees. I could see there was writing on the walls as I held up my blue light up. I turned around, holding my light above my head to make sure Miranda was still with me. She must have seen the fear on my face. "I am coming with you, but we need to hurry and make it back to where we came in before the water fills up."

"Are you sure she is down here? What if we don't get to her in time? Is there another way out other than where we came in?"

"Shhh! We are getting closer to the portal," she whispered, "When we get there you may have to cross over into another dimension and bring your mother back. But don't worry, you are much stronger than you think and you should be able to accomplish this."

"Okay. Anything else you want to share with me, so last minute?"

"Yes, if the tunnels fill up with water you may have to stay on the other side until the waters drain out, otherwise we will all drown."

"Are you coming with me to the other side?"

"Not exactly. I am not physically down here with you. I am just a teleported vision. I didn't come down here with you in body, just in spirit. If I can teleport across dimension I will go with you, but that is very hard to do and I have not been able to master that skill yet."

"You mean to tell me that you are not really here?" I swiped my arm out at her and vapors divided her body into two parts. The vision flickered and the vapor returned to show her full form again. "Unbelievable, just when I think I can trust someone, they lie to me!"

"You really need to hurry, not only for your mother's life, but your own as well," she said, pointing down to the water that was almost mid-thigh now. I turned, using my arms and swaying my body to help push through the water. I rounded the curve and peeked into the large opening ahead, keeping my light over my head. The room filled with water about waist high.

There were six tunnels that led out of the round room. The floor in the middle was glowing green under the water. I shimmied into the room and the water began to come alive. It swirled like a drain, pulling in the middle, creating a cylinder that rose up towering over me reaching to the ceiling. The wall of water glowed a brighter green, filling the room with light. I squeezed my palm, extinguishing the blue light.

The water still rose around me as my shirt began to float up around my sides, pulling the right in the same direction as the water cylinder. Bracing myself with my knees bent, I stood with my legs wide to keep my balance in the increasing swift current. "Mama?"

Over the rushing sound of the water, I heard my mama's voice. "Arielle? Is that you, Arielle? Can you see me?"

"Mama? Where are you? I can't see you, but I can hear you!"

"Arielle, get out of here!" she cried loudly over the water pulling me towards the cylinder of water.

"I can't leave you, Mama. You are all I have left!" With the water up to my shoulders, I lost my footing. Frantically, I tried to swim, but the wet clothes and tennis shoes weighted me down. Keeping my head above water, I swirled around the green pulsing cylinder of water. Swishing by the wall of water, I ran my hands along the solid shimmering glassy waves. Spinning around in circles, I turned my focus inside the wall. I could see Mama. She was sitting on the floor at the bottom of the room completely dry and all alone. "Mama! I see you! But I don't know how to get to you."

"Arielle, don't come across the portal. It is too dangerous!"

I felt a hand on my shoulder while drifting; it was Miranda. "You can do this. You have the power inside of you. Just believe in yourself. I can see greatness in your soul. Your father is with you, guiding you. The portal is too strong. I don't have the ability to go with you. God be with you, child." She evaporated before I could even respond or ask any questions.

"Here goes nothing," I called to Mama. I placed both hands on the wall and dug deep with my fingers, trying to grab a hold of something. Nothing happened and I swirled around the cylinder wall again. "God, I have the power, but not the knowledge. Please guide me!" My head clouded with dizziness as the water rose fast. My head was only about two feet from the ceiling. I couldn't go back now as I started to lose courage. The ceiling got closer and closer to my face.

Placing my hands on the wall, I saw the green light began to flicker off and on, leaving me in moments of complete darkness. Pressing my eyes closed hard, I flicked out two blue globes of light in each palm, pressing them hard into the wall. My body turned from the pressure while my feet trailed behind me. Water splashed, covering my head. Pulling my hands away, I coughed away the water and opened my eyes to see a good indent in the wall where I had applied pressure.

Taking a deep breath, I dug in as hard as I could into the wall. A small crack was starting to form. "It's working, Mama! I am coming!" I only had a foot of airspace left, but I kept on pressing. Each rotation the crack became a little bigger. I was getting closer to breaking into the other side and also running out of air. The next rotation I took a deep breath and fully submerged into the rainwater.

I could hear the muffled cries of my mama yelling my name. The rush of the water was so strong I missed the crack on the first rotation. The second spin my arm pushed through, but only my arm was on the other side and I couldn't make it through with my body. Pounding with my free palm, the crack began to grow. I started to feel light-headed; I desperately needed air. Blinking under water a white glow floated towards me. It was Breeze! With one forceful head butt, the wall cracked and we both went tumbling into the cylinder. Falling about eight feet down to the ground, he broke my fall with a groan. I scrambled to my feet to place my hand on him to make sure he was all right. Mama called to me as I stooped over Breeze.

"Arielle, you shouldn't have come. I don't know how we are going to escape this hell!"

I threw my arms around her and hugged her so hard I almost knocked us both over. "Mama, how could I not come and find you?" I cried.

She patted my back, cupping my face in her hands. "Thank you for finding me," she continued. "What happened to the dog?"

My eyes filled with tears. I didn't want her to see my crying. I swallowed hard and flicked the tears away before letting her go. "I don't know where Breeze went, but I am sure he is fine. He is pretty amazing," I told her while facing her and holding her arms in my hands, not letting her go. "I am so glad I found you. How did this happen to you?"

"The last thing I remember is getting into a cab, a black Lincoln after meeting a few friends out, but the driver didn't take me home. She brought me to the Jean Lafitte Blacksmith Bar, and she sprayed my face with some type of mist. I am ready to wake up from this dream."

"Has anyone or anything tried to harm you?"

"No one has hurt me, but some of the other creatures coming into this dream have been tortured. Their screams are unbearable. This must be a very wicked place. I am so mentally exhausted; can you wake me up now?" I nodded to agree with everything she had said.

The winds picking up around us caused our hair to fly around. There were haunting sounds that whispered as they circled around, "Okay, Mama, we are going to figure this out together and get out of here." I took my focus off her, looking at our surroundings. I couldn't tell if the water on the other side of the wall was emptying out of the tunnel or not. It was a chance to try to break back through right away, not knowing what lay on the other side. But staying here, our welcome might run out quickly too.

"The area that you fell from is still open at the top, but I don't know how we can get up there. It is too high for us to jump and there is no way to climb."

"Did you notice anything while you were here that seems friendly? Someone or something that might be able to help us get out of here?" I quizzed her.

"There were a few flashes of white lights, but nothing has really made contact with me since I have been here. It is almost like I am invisible to all the creatures, which by the looks of them, I am happy with being ignored to all of them!"

"There has to be another way to get out of here than that hole at the top," I said. "How did the other creatures come in and out of here?"

"They just passed through. They didn't break in like you did. Well, if this is my dream, then why don't we just walk through the wall?" she asked me as she teetered a little from the strong winds continuing to grow. She grabbed my arm, starting to walk to the wall.

"Mama, I don't think this is just a dream, but we can try," I said, holding onto her tightly around her waist as we bumped into the wall with no success.

"Now for plan B. We call for help. Hello? Anyone out there that can help us?" Mama called.

The winds stopped abruptly, and all the whispers and chatter silenced. A few creatures draped in dark cloth started to drift towards us. We were up against the wall with nowhere to run. "Maybe I shouldn't have asked in such a nonspecific way? Anyone else out there that can help us?" she shouted beyond the slowly approaching figures.

Positioning myself in front of Mama, I held out my palms just like the night with Dixie shooting out a blot of blue lightning. It came in contact with the first creature, which squealed like a pig as its leather-like arms failed under the draping cloth. I waited to see if it would fall to the ground. It just stood there disoriented and not moving. Seeing something in our favor, I blasted the next creature and it froze in place too, after a long squeal. I didn't take time to see Mama's reaction I just kept blasting anything threatening us. We had a pile of frozen beasts that soon they couldn't even get around each other to reach us. Mama paused me to ask, "Why don't you try your blaster on the wall?"

"Good idea, Mama," I said. Turning to face the wall, I pointed my glowing ray of light and etched out a door frame, tracing over it again and again.

"Good job, honey, keep going!" Mama cheered, watching me chisel away at the thick wall.

"I just hope all the water is gone on the other side of the wall, otherwise we might be in worse shape than we are now." I told her, keeping my focus on the task. My left arm started to tingle and the sensation crept up my shoulder into my neck. Shrugging my shoulder, I tried to push the feeling way, thinking it was maybe a backlash of the blot coming from my palms. The feeling increased and moved across to my other shoulder and down that arm, turning into a numbing pain.

"Arielle, they are on you!" Mama shouted as she lunged towards the creature that was wrapping his dark brown leather-like fingers around my neck. The creature raised its arm, causing Mama to fly back before she even made contact with him. She landed square on her butt. The creature let me go and went after Mama, who was dazed and trying to get up off the floor.

Keeping the beams on, I rotated away from the wall, blasting everything near us, including the one that was going after Mama. I kept the blue light focused on him as he squealed and began to glow and pulse an orange color, exploding into tiny shards of red flames then extinguishing. I felt like I was in a video game having to destroy an entire realm of bad guys, and as soon as one was destroyed another one appeared. I couldn't work on the wall and destroy the demons at the same time. I was getting tired and frustrated, but I had to keep going. "Mama, I don't know how to get us out of here."

"Maybe it is time to pray a little harder?"

"You work on that while I do something constructive over here," I said a little too condescendingly.

"Arielle, where is your faith?" She knelt down right there in the middle of all this chaos and folded her hands and began to pray. *She really must think we are in a dream!* I thought to myself. I kept destroying and she kept on praying. Between the two of us something was bound to change. She placed her hands on the door frame I chiseled out. It began to crack. I paused to look at her, but she didn't even look up. She kept praying. The wall's cracks started to light up a deep purple color. I could see beams of the purple light starting to shine through the tiny holes developing.

Breaking her concentration, I called, "Mama, you might want to move. The wall is coming down!"

Her eyes popped open as she carefully rose to her feet, standing next to the frame. It caved in towards us, opening the portal into our realm. Demons started chanting, moving quickly to the doorway. I gave one long semi-circle blast and grabbed Mama's wrist, pulling her through the makeshift doorway. Miranda was there and the water lapped at her ankles. "Quickly, we need to close the portal!" She motioned for me to stand next to her.

"Mama, get behind us," I told her as I positioned myself by her side taking a boxer's stance with my palms facing the wall. "What do we do now?"

"We need to take down the wall. Destroy all of it."

Following her lead, we crossed beams trying to crack down the wall to close up the door. A demon scampered into our world. She shot it down, and it squealed until it exploded. The wall was starting to break down just as three more demons crossed over. I got one and she got another, but the third escaped, scurrying around Mama into the darkness of a tunnel. "Just keep working," Miranda commanded.

"It is starting to come down! Mama, take cover in one of the tunnels."

The wall burst as it came tumbling down. Every single piece dissolved into the floor as if it never was even there. The room was silent other than the sloshing of our feet on the wet brick ground.

"And that was an impressive portal!" Miranda said as she extinguished her beams.

Mama emerged from a tunnel, saying, "This dream has gone on just long enough. I am ready to wake up."

"Ms. Mathis, if only it was a dream this would have been a very vivid one."

"Mama, we have a lot to talk about, but later. Let's get above ground." Making our way back, I asked Miranda, "What about that one demon that escaped into our world?"

"Let's just hope that it was one with little experience and we can catch him. I will work on that first thing tomorrow casting luring spells. Don't worry I am good at tracking demons."

"Just don't let this one get a hold of you like the last one," I said, biting my bottom lip, wishing I wouldn't have said that out loud to her. "I am sorry. I am not trying to be rude, especially since you came to help us out after all."

"Point taken, child," she said with a little annoyance in her voice.

Mama was quiet the whole time until we got out of the tunnel stepping out onto the sidewalk by Lafitte's Blacksmith Bar. She asked, "Can I wake up now?"

"Mama, this isn't a dream. You have been missing since last night. Don't you remember?"

"No, honey, I am sure I made it home last night. This is all a dream."

Ignoring her confusion, I asked Miranda, "How long were we down in the tunnel?"

Big E, who was standing on the sidewalk waiting for our emergence, said, "It is only been about thirty minutes since you left our home, typical rainstorm."

"Surely we were gone for more than thirty minutes."

204

"Yes, in our standard of time we were. Portals have a way of causing a refraction in time. You may come out and it has been a year later, or less than a minute. I don't recommend you cross over again. You just can't determine how your time will shift when you leave this realm." I nodded to show I understood her. "Please stop by and we will make an appointment for afternoon tea and discuss this in length. I would like to have you refresh my mind of what exactly happened in my home today."

Miranda didn't remember anything either. "Yes, Ms. LaTour, I will do that. And thank you for your gracious help today," I said and gave her a slight bow to show my appreciation.

"Excuse me," Mama said, trying to get my attention without being rude, resting her hand on my arm and pointing with the other hand. "Arielle, that is the black Lincoln that picked me up last night. Can we finish our ride home now? Maybe that will wake me up."

Miranda's eyes narrowed as she followed the direction Mama pointed in and gasped, holding her hand delicately to her chest. "That is my car. It is certainly not a cab!"

"Mama, let's just go home." Mama nodded as she started over to the car. "We can just walk home from here."

"Let us drop you home," Big E insisted.

Mama and I stepped into the car with Big E driving. Miranda took the front passenger seat. Miranda gave him directions to our house before I even could open my mouth. We only lived a few blocks away, but it was an awkward few minutes. Before Mama opened her door, Miranda flicked her long nails in Mama's direction and a sizzling mist drifted over Mama's eyes, causing them to roll back into her head then twisting around to face me. "This will clear her mind and she won't remember anything that just happened. It is easier this way and how your papa has wanted it for many years.

We will talk later or hopefully he has written about me in his book. No more talk for now."

Mark came running out of the house with Charlie close behind him, both saying at the same time, "What happened?"

CHAPTER TWENTY-TWO
Wiped Clean

Mama wrapped her arms around Mark's neck and gave him a big kiss on the cheek. "It is nice to see you, son."

"You too, Mama," he said, giving me a concerned look as I gave him a motion of cutting at the neck to tell him don't say anything! He nodded to me.

"Give me my purse so I can pay the cab driver."

"I got it covered," I said, handing Big E some cash from my pocket. Whispering to Charlie, "When did you get here?"

He whispered back, "I just got here. Mark called me as soon as you darted out of the house," He glanced at his rugged black watch. "That was about thirty-five to forty minutes ago. I rushed to get here."

Extending his hand, Big E played along, taking the money and asking in a joking tone, "Do you need any change?"

"You can keep the change." Mama waved at big E.

"Of course, ma'am." He bent forward and gave her a tiny salute, scooting off. Miranda didn't even get out of the car, how rude.

Mama asked, "Charlie, you will stay for dinner, won't you? And what are you two whispering about over there?"

He smiled at me, answering her, but ignoring the second question, "Yes, ma'am, I would be happy to say for dinner."

"Such a gentleman this one!" Mama said, then smacked Mark in the back of head, "Why aren't all your friends this pleasant?' We all chuckled going into the house. Looking around the kitchen with a frown, Mama asked Mark and Charlie, "You boys don't mind running to the store, do you?"

I hopped in the shower to get cleaned up. Wrapping my arms around my chest, I placed my hands on my shoulders feeling millions of pinholes where my wings were. I ran my fingers over them, wondering when I would get wings again. I wasn't ready to die for my wings, but they sure were exhilarating. It was refreshing to slide into some clean clothes. I blinked twice at the mirror, checking my mascara and made a kiss face, inspecting my shimmering lip gloss.

My peripheral vision began to fade. What now? Focusing in the middle of the mirror where I could see, a blue orb appeared, relaxing me. Demons circled around the blue orb lunging and attacking it. The orb couldn't fight off the amount of demons and flickered and grew dim. I slammed my left palm against the glass in anger. The mirror smashed, shattering into a spider web. I thought my hand would go through like a portal. Small drops of blood beaded up over the cuts that covered a good bottom portion of my palm. Glancing up into the mirror, I saw everything had vanished and my full vision returned. This warning made me realize things were far from over and my world was now changed forever.

I used a hand towel to stop the bleeding by pressing it on my palm. There must be some pieces of glass still in there because the pressure made the cuts sting. My face frowned, seeing that the mirror got the worst end of the deal for sure.

Studying my hand, I gently ran my fingernail over the cut to try to pull out some glass. "I slipped on the wet floor and caught myself with my palm in the mirror." She examined it closely to see if there were any glass chards in my palm, using tweezers she pulled a few shards out. She cleaned the wound very tenderly with soapy water and wrapped a mesh gauze bandage on it in total silence.

After she washed herself and went back to finish up dinner, we all sat down for dinner. Mama had made meatloaf and garlic mashed potatoes. This was one of my favorite meals; I was smiles with my meal and my family. After dinner, I carried the dishes to the sink as best I could with my new injury. Mark bumped me out of the way, saying accusingly, "You must have done that on purpose so you don't have to do the dishes." He pointed to my hand with the scrubbing brush.

I didn't have any witty comebacks so I just agreed with him. "Yeah you must be right."

The phone rang in the kitchen. "Hello? Hi, Nicole. Yes, he is right here, hold up a minute." I pointed to the phone as Mark was just getting started on the dishes. He flicked his fingers into the sink before taking the phone.

Charlie came to take over. I pretended to look at my bandaged palm, but secretly watched him. It took him only a minute to quick rinse and load the dishwasher. Left alone in the kitchen, I walked over to him and took his hand. I didn't have the courage to look up at his eyes yet, but he didn't pull away either. I placed his hand over my racing heart, letting our eyes meet.

I spoke quietly, "Thank you for everything. I was so lost and you somehow knew everything that I needed."

He responded, "I think I know one more thing that you need from me." He took both his hands and gently held my head, slowly leaning in. I could feel his warm breath as my eyes closed ready for the kiss. A throat cleared loudly, interrupting us. My eyes popped open as I was jolted back from my daydream. Charlie was still by the sink finishing up the dishes and I was planted on the chair. In unison our heads turned to the kitchen door, and there was Mama with her hands on both hips.

With her chin jutted out and looking at us sidewise, she proclaimed, "Who is up for a game of Gin Rummy?"

Charlie dried his hands on the front of his jeans and responded to Mama, "My apologies, but I should be on my way."

She flagged her hands above her head. "You are not going home to the swamp this late at night. Get yourself settled in a room away from Arielle's."

I laughed nervously and then drew a serious face.

He nodded. "Thank you."

Mark came back into the kitchen, and with an extended hand, he clapped hands with Charlie and they went in for a half hug. "I have to go home to the wife and kiddo. And Charlie, thanks for making Mom think I have a least one decent friend."

Charlie winked saying, "Of course, no problem."

Mama said to Mark, "Tell your little family I said hello and I love them."

Mark gave me a little punch on the arm and said, "Please be careful." I nodded.

I told her, "Do you mind if we do cards another night?"

"Of course, honey. It has been a long day for me too."

Charlie asked, "Could I shower and get cleaned up?"

"Let me show you where everything is in the house so you can make yourself comfortable," Mama said, leading him upstairs for a peaceful night' sleep.

The next morning, I hid my smile behind my coffee cup, very glad he was in our lives and everyone was getting along so well. Once Charlie was packed up, he said to me, "I hope to see you again soon." He leaned in and whispered in my ear, "Thanksgiving. I expect you to come visit me."

Mama handed him a bag of leftovers to take home and he said, "Thank you."

"You are welcome," she said, patting him on the arm and going back to the kitchen.

As I stood in the courtyard doorway, he stole a quick kiss before he left. I was left there with my fingers lingering over my lips watching him walk away to his Jeep, Breeze on the street following behind him. I guess he was going to watch over Charlie for a while.

The Thanksgiving holiday break was fast approaching, "So Mama, are we still going to the beach for Thanksgiving this summer?"

"I talked to Mark and Nicole and the plan is to go on Wednesday to the beach and come home on Sunday," she said.

"Okay, I didn't know if this would be hard to do since we have been going for so long and Dad isn't going to be with us this year."

"I know, honey, I thought about how it will never be the same." She swept the tears away with her index fingers.

"I feel the same way, Mama," I said. "So that gives me Friday night till Wednesday to visit with Aunt Nina and Charlie? I would like to see Charlie over the break and his Aunt Nina, so I might go to the camp and meet up with him."

I broke the silence. "I am not a kid anymore. I won't be stupid either."

She finally said, "I don't like it, but I can't stop you either. Try to be back by Tuesday so we don't leave so late on Wednesday for the beach, please."

"Why don't you go stay these few days at Mark and Nicole's house, so you are not here without me? It would make me feel better if you went there. You could spend more time with your only grand kiddo!" I said, nodding to convince her even more of the great idea that I just unloaded on her. She nodded as a smile formed across her face.

Friday couldn't have come sooner. At noon, I scooted home to a very quiet house to grab my things and chuck my books. The spirits had been very distant since the incident with Miranda and the tunnels. Even on Halloween night they had been silent. I reached back to make sure the door was locked. I didn't look back at the house I put the bag on my back, helmet on, and cranked the motorcycle. I parked the motorcycle under the camp and pulled off my helmet and tried to fluff my hair as best I could and walked over to Charlie, all smiles.

"Hey, you," he said as he extended his arms out towards me for an embrace.

I said, "Hey back at you." It was nice to be in his comforting arms. Once we were at his camp, his cousin and Aunt Nina were there preparing dinner.

She gave me a huge hug and pinched my cheeks. "I am so proud of you and can't wait to hear the whole story."

I waved a hello to Nick who was stirring something on the stove. He threw his head back with a nod to say "Hey". He wasn't much of a talker. Dinner was nice. We chatted about the alligator season and the field trips that had come this year. Things were going great for them. I was itching to tell Aunt Nina everything, but I waited for the right time. After dinner Nick made his way to his camp just a few waterways downstream. I stood close to Charlie, slightly leaning into him while helping him with the dishes. Aunt Nina watched us from the table. Once we were done I sat down next to her.

She said, "Y'all make a good pair."

I blushed and told her, "Thank you. I think so too."

She listened as I rattled off all the descriptions of what happened from the trap door, the room, the defeat of Miranda and

212

how she didn't remember anything until she read my palm. And how there are tunnels under the city of New Orleans!

"I haven't gone to talk to Miranda after everything yet," I said. "Do you think that she is still possessed?" I asked.

Aunt Nina took her time to answer this. "It is hard to tell. From the sounds of it, everything points to the side that she is free from the demons, especially since she came to help you rescue your mama. Demons are a little cunning, but that seems to be more out of the realm of what they would normally do," Aunt Nina advised. "You don't need to have any contact with her if you don't want to."

"I was so curious to talk to her, yet so afraid. I don't know what I really need to say to her now that Mama is back. She acted like she really knew you well too. You must have a past with each other?"

Aunt Nina said, "If you need it for closure then you do it now, the longer you wait the more you won't do it. Yes, we went to grade school together. We both knew we each had powers, but she dropped out of high school and tried to get me to do the same. We just went down different paths."

Aunt Nina and I stayed up till about two in the morning just talking about things we have experienced in our lives. She had so many stories that gave me the chills. But nothing compared to when I told her, "I shot bolts of light out of my hands! But what was even greater, I had WINGS!" I squealed. "They all are gone. Even the pinholes have healed where the angels placed them into my shoulders."

"Wow, that must have been exhilarating. These wings and bolts of light is new territory to me and I don't know of anyone able to do such a thing," she said, "I must do some research in my books and talk with Father Beau. I am interested in figuring out what you are capable of doing," she said with a yawn.

*****

Charlie said as he poured me a cup of coffee, "Aunt Nina was already on her way home before you rose to do some research and contact Father Verum and Father Beau."

The next few days were relaxed and fun wandering around the alligator farm. Monday afternoon Charlie broke the trance of absorbing the world around me. "Tomorrow maybe we should take a trip over to Aunt Nina's to see what she is up to? I'm surprised she hasn't made it back here yet and you are leaving soon, right?"

"I was thinking it was odd too, she hasn't been back yet either... I hate that she doesn't have a phone so I can call her. I can't imagine not having a house phone."

"You could really old school it and write her a letter."

"Ugh. I am doing enough writing in the book that I am keeping, but I guess you are right. Can you get me her address? Hey, wait a minute, are you joking with me? Y'all don't have mailboxes out here!"

He just shrugged, laughing at me, watching me, processing the thought of a mailman via boat delivering the mail out in the swamps, "We have P.O. boxes. You know, we still have to pay our electric and water bills."

"Oh yeah! That makes sense. I guess that was my blond moment for the day!" We spent the rest of the evening sitting outside and talking about ourselves to each other. My cheeks hurt from smiling I was having so much fun. Several hours later sleep finally won and I had a quiet slumber.

As my eyes fluttered open, I thought to myself again, *There is something amazing about waking up to brewing coffee. It makes me feel so spoiled.*

"Arielle, you getting up?" I heard Charlie calling from the door.

"Make me!" I fussed back.

"Okay, I am going to Aunt Nina's without you. Did that work?"

Opening the door, I gave him a one-eyed glare. "You wouldn't dare!" I pushed past him and bustled to the bathroom to hurry to get ready. Walking into the kitchen, Charlie stood with both hands behind his back and a big smile. "What are you up to?"

"Merry Christmas, early," he said, pulling from behind him a box wrapped in comic strip newspaper, gently placing it on the kitchen table. I sat down, pressing my hands across the box to let my fingers find the gap to tear the paper. Dropping the paper on the floor, I shook the top of the box to release it from the bottom onto the kitchen table. There was white tissue paper that I pulled back and saw a soft light pink garment inside. Lifting the item out, it had some texture and lace to it around the bottom.

"This is really cool vest," I said.

He explained, "With Aunt Nina's help it is an enchantment vest to keep you protected."

"This is the most amazing present I think anyone has given to me."

"I sewed it myself, but if it needs to be altered Aunt Nina can do that part."

I got up and threw my arms around him and gave him a long hug. "I love it." We pulled back and he gently kissed my lips.

Looking deeply into my green eyes, he said, "I want your heart to be protected, so I am the only one that can touch it."

I sighed and gave him a dreamy smile. I said, "You have a hold of my heart right now." I slid the vest on and wrapped my arms around, hugging myself, "I can't wait for Aunt Nina to see it on me. It fits great," I said and did a little twirl. "I didn't know you knew how to sew too. Is there anything you don't do?"

He chuckled ignoring my question. "Let's get going."

CHAPTER TWENTY-THREE

Aunt Nina's Book

As we approached, I saw Aunt Nina sitting on her porch with two angels surrounding her. The translucent feathers wrapped around her faded as our boat hit the dock. Lost in her deep meditation, she didn't look up from the book she held in her hands. The sounds of thunder rolling in the distance caught our attention as we walked up the stairs to her porch. Charlie placed his hand on her shoulder to give her a little shake. "Aunt Nina?" She didn't respond…

"Charlie? Wake her up." A tear escaped, rolling down my pink cheek.

Charlie turned and wrapped his arms around me as he sniffled, trying to hold back his tears. "Arielle do you think you can make it back in the pirogue without me and call the coroner's office?"

"I think so."

"I need you right now," he said, lifting my chin so our tear-filled eyes met.

"Yes, I understand. I will wait for them at your house and bring them here?"

"Yes, please go quickly. Here take this with you. She would want you to have it." He handed me the book that was on her lap…

"Mama, I don't think I will be home today," I said with my voice cracking.

"Arielle, what is going on, sweetie? What happened? Is everyone all right?"

"We are fine, but Charlie's aunt... is not... I just got off the phone with the coroner's office. Aunt Nina passed away. We found her at her camp this morning. I'm sorry, but I have to go. They just arrived and I am going to take them over to her camp now. I think I should stay one more night with Charlie."

"Okay, Arielle, Tell Charlie we are here if he needs anything."

Charlie was speaking to the coroner while I walked around her property and the tabby cat appeared. I knelt down on both legs and sat. The tabby put his front paws on my knees and leaned in to touch his nose on my nose and evaporated, "Bye, kitty." I let the tears flow down my face looking to the sky asking, God, *why do you keep taking people from me? I need her more than you do!*

Charlie came down the path. Seeing me on the ground, he ran over. "Are you okay? Did you fall?"

"No, I was saying goodbye to Aunt Nina's tabby cat. And just didn't get up yet. I am fine. Just a little shocked and pissed off." Charlie helped me up to my feet. "How are you so calm?"

"Arielle, I have dealt with so much death I just remind myself we will all be together again. And when that happens it will be for eternity."

"Ugh. I know all that, but I have trouble seeing it as a positive right now. All I feel is hurt, loss, and anger."

"I feel those things too, but I can see past those feelings. You can too, it takes time."

"I called Mama and said I won't be home today." Charlie opened his mouth to object. "It is already settled."

The rest of the afternoon was a blur. Nick came over right away and the guys sat on the porch in silence for about an hour and then Nick got up, hugged Charlie, and left. I joined Charlie, sitting where Nick was. "The seat is still warm," I said to Charlie because I didn't know what else to talk about.

He nodded. "All the girls say Nick has a hot butt." Breaking the sadness with laughter, Charlie reached for my hand to lock our fingers together. "Arielle, I am glad you are here, I am sorry you had to see her like that."

"She looked like she was meditating and so peaceful."

"That is how I want you to remember her. There is a whole lot of ugly in this world. Try to always remember the beautiful."

"I will try," I said, leaving him on the porch to watch the sunset deep in his thoughts.

Charlie returned me home to my family's camp and we shared an extra-long kiss at my parents' camp.

"When am I going to see you again?" I asked Charlie.

"I will let you know once I make her arrangements."

I gave him the signature motorcycle wave as I pulled onto the road heading home, arm extended pointing with two fingers in his direction. He smiled and flashed a peace sign.

*****

The overcast weather matched my somber mood for Aunt Nina's funeral on that Monday. It was already 10 a.m. when I pulled myself out of bed. I poured coffee in a small white Styrofoam cup and hollered upstairs to Mama, "I am going to walk to the church."

"Okay, honey, you may want to take an umbrella with you... Doesn't the service start at noon?" she called from the top of the stairs.

Looking up at her, I saw her hair was still wet from her shower. She wouldn't be ready to go right now anyway. "Yes, ma'am. Do you want me to save you a seat by Charlie?"

"No, I will sit with my friends in the back."

"I will see you there. Love you," I called. Stepping outside our house into the courtyard, I took a swig of the steaming coffee, standing there absorbing the grossness of the weather. The low clouds created a blanket of mist over the whole city. An umbrella wouldn't protect you from the mist. It was everywhere in the air. Carefully I lifted my cross-body bag over my right shoulder, steadying my coffee. St. Louis Cathedral was a short seven-minute walk. This wouldn't fill the gap in time before it started. I figured I could spend some time in Jackson Square or maybe search for Father Beau and Father Verum before the service started as they were both leading her service. My stroll took about twenty minutes to arrive at Jackson Square.

My black shiny patent leather with a slight heel glistened with the mist covering them. I opted to wear black pantyhose to hide my stark white legs that were not covered below my knees from my pencil-thin dark charcoal skirt. Shrugging my shoulders, I tried to get the silky blouse with the ruffles around the collar to not stick to my skin but not much luck. Carefully stepping into the square, tons of people all dressed in black milled around, none that I recognized. I wandered around, finding a seat on an old cement bench under a large oak tree.

Pulling out Papa's book, I pretended to read as I watched the people congregating in the square chattering about the funeral and sharing stories about Nina. Glancing at the clock atop the cathedral, the time was only 11:00. It was still too early to go inside. I contained the tears that wanted to flow free and put the book back in my bag. I stood to wander around the perimeter of the park to look at the vendors selling their goods. Hopeful, I would find either one of the Fathers.

I entered the gates, pausing to glance up. Six of the gray birds perched at the very top of the cathedral. Giving a low growl as I glared daggers, I thought *Why are they even here?* My view was obstructed from an arm waving in front of me. Bringing my gaze down to ground level, I saw Father Verum dressed in his traditional black attired accompanied with a stark white Roman collar over the middle of his neck. My face softened. "Hi, Father, I am so glad to see you again."

"Hi, Arielle, I really would like to talk to you before you leave today. There are some questions I would like to ask in private about my last visit with Ms. Nina."

"I would like to chat with you as well."

"Do you want to meet in the back courtyard after mass? Oh, and do you know who ended up with Ms. Nina's personal book?"

"Yes, I have it. Charlie gave it to me."

"Very good. I just wanted to make sure it was safe. Do you have it with you or it is at your home?"

"I have it with me," I said as I started to pull it out of my bag to show him. He quickly placed his hand over mine, pushing the book back into the bag, looking around to see if anyone was near.

"We should do this later."

Surprised at his actions, I just agreed with him nodding yes repeatedly, "Sure... no problem... I will meet you out back after."

He nodded and turned to walk over to the side entrance, leaving me standing there. Several people walked around me and into the cathedral. I followed.

Finding Charlie in the second row from the front, I sat next to him and whispered, "Who are all these people? Are most of them family?"

"No, most of them are people she has helped. She had a strong presence in the swamp community and the city. She touched many people's lives."

I nodded, knowing how much she had changed my life and how much I would miss her. Listening to the soft chatter around us with the lack of prelude music, I recalled the last time we spoke. I should have asked her more questions. *Like how to open her book!* I have learned with Papa's book if I lock it, only I can open it without the hyssop oil. I carried all three books in my jet-black cross body leather bag rested on my left hip.

I reached for Charlie's hand and gave it a squeeze. He squeezed back as we sat there in silence. The service was very traditional and long, especially the communion, because there were rows of people standing in the back of the church with no room in the pews. Towards the end, I whispered again to Charlie. "I will meet you at the grave site. I have to meet someone in the courtyard." He nodded *Yes* without looking towards me.

As I stepped out into the courtyard to wait for Father Verum, the bells clanged, indicating it was already 3:00 pm. The muggy weather was starting to turn cool outside as the day crept on. I rubbed my arms to take the chill off them. Shuffling on the slippery bricks, I stood next to the building, gazing out into the quiet, still courtyard. There was a rustling in the bushes over to the left side. Stooping down, I looked to see what kind of animal or bird was making such a fuss. Two eyes peered out at me as I squinted to get a better look, straining my neck to look under the thick banana leaves. Coaxing it out, I made a few small clicking sounds with my tongue as it shuffled completely out of view.

Still squatting down, I moved my bag to my backside to keep it out of the way as I kept my balance, shuffling over to peek into a hole in the leaves. The winds started to violently swirl around me, causing me to teeter a little. Putting my hand down on the damp
222

ground, I steadied myself. Then I felt a blow to the back of my head. My world went dark.

Born in NOLA, but primarily raised in Slidell, Louisiana I love the lure of Voodoo and other haunted folklore of this area. I am a believer in the trinity and evil spirits. I do not practice Voodoo. I am a fiction writer with a flair for the paranormal. My hobbies other than writing include creating art such as pottery, painting, vintage button jewelry and crafts. I often create, listening to Christian music. I am joyfully married and we live with two little fluffy pups. I enjoy the beach and an excellent cup of coffee. Volunteering is also important to me. I am an active member of Junior Auxiliary of Slidell. I have been blessed with much in my life and want to give back to the children in my community.

Made in the USA
Lexington, KY
28 November 2019

Made in the USA
Lexington, KY
28 November 2019

57805466R00141